Kyra spun ... **her sides. "** ... **background** ... **task force member or just the ones you don't want to work with?"**

Jake clasped a hand on the back of his neck, and for the first time she noticed the weariness in his handsome face, the lines on the sides of his mouth etched deep, the hazel eyes dark and unfathomable.

"Is that what you think? That I don't want to work with you? I invited you to survey the video footage with me today. I drove you to the murder scene last night."

She blinked her eyes. And she might've just messed up.

"Besides," he sighed, "I didn't discover who you were by looking into your background, although I tried. Your name and ID change are pretty thorough. There is nothing online that links you to that little girl."

"Then how'd you find out and why were you digging into my past?"

THE SETUP

Carol Ericson

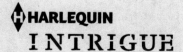

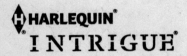

ISBN-13: 978-1-335-40165-6

The Setup

Recycling programs
for this product may
not exist in your area.

Harlequin Enterprises ULC
22 Adelaide St. West, 40th Floor
Toronto, Ontario M5H 4E3, Canada
www.Harlequin.com

Printed in U.S.A.

Carol Ericson is a bestselling, award-winning author of more than forty books. She has an eerie fascination for true-crime stories, a love of film noir and a weakness for reality TV, all of which fuel her imagination to create her own tales of murder, mayhem and mystery. To find out more about Carol and her current projects, please visit her website at www.carolericson.com, "where romance flirts with danger."

Visit the Author Profile page at Harlequin.com.

CAST OF CHARACTERS

Jake McAllister—This LAPD homicide detective is leading a task force to find a serial killer who is copying the MO of a killer from twenty years ago. As if he doesn't have enough on his plate, Kyra Chase, a therapist and victims' rights advocate, has been assigned to his task force, complicating not only his investigation, but his life.

Kyra Chase—A therapist with deep, dark secrets, she has her own reasons for wanting to be on McAllister's serial killer task force, but her attraction to the sexy, no-nonsense detective is a distraction she doesn't need.

Roger Quinn—A retired LAPD homicide detective with one failure on his record—his inability to catch the serial killer known as The Player. He's tried to make up for it by protecting one of The Player's victims for twenty years.

Billy Crouch—Jake's partner is the levelheaded one of the duo, but he has his own traumas to overcome to be able to do his job.

Matt Dugan—Kyra's foster brother knows a lot about her, maybe too much for his own safety.

The Copycat Player—A serial killer who follows all the rules of the game—except one.

Prologue

Rule number four. The victim should never be someone you know.

He screwed up his face and squinted at the girl curled up in the back seat of his car. He didn't really know Kelsey. Seeing her around, knowing her name—that didn't count, did it? He hadn't known Shelby or Marissa, either. They didn't know *his* name, had barely given him the time of day.

Through the slits of his eyes, he could almost imagine Kelsey smiling at him. That was better than the last look she gave him. He smiled back.

A rustling noise from the trailhead wiped the smile off his face and made his heart pound—not in a good way, not the way it had raced the first time he'd put his hands on Kelsey. He held his breath until he saw the flash of a squirrel's tail as it hopped out of a tree. The animal turned its head in his direction and pierced him with its beady eyes. He stomped his foot in the squirrel's direction, sending the creature up another tree.

He hooked his arms beneath Kelsey's and dragged her out of the car, the heels of her boots hitting the soft ground. He'd place her off the trail but not too far off. Someone needed to discover his handiwork before the animals got to her. Seemed like he'd made that mistake with Shelby. He'd already scoped out this location, had visited it a few times.

His running shoes scuffed through the dry debris that littered the trail as he pulled her deadweight several feet. He stopped and wiped a bead of sweat from his face with his arm. Kelsey was a lot heavier in death, but he'd discovered this with the others. This wasn't his first rodeo. It was his third rodeo. He giggled at his pun.

Another ten feet, and he located his spot—her spot now—and let Kelsey's upper body drop with a huffing sound on the comfy cushion of leaves, twigs and berries beneath the tree, one arm crossing her body. The scent of pine and citrus tingled in his nose, and he inhaled the clean smell. Maybe he should take up hiking. Being out here made him feel good. He glanced at Kelsey—or maybe this was what made him feel good.

Now the annoying work part started. He crouched beside the body and plucked at the sleeve of her shirt to move her arm to her side. He lined up her legs, straight and together, the toes of her boots pointing skyward. He brushed some dirt from the leg of her jeans.

The bruises ringing her throat created an unfortunate purple necklace, but he didn't have a gun, and a knife would've left a mess of blood in his car. He liked blood, but not if he had to get rid of it.

When he'd killed those little animals, the blood didn't matter. Nobody was running around investigating the deaths of possums. He snorted and a wisp of Kelsey's blond hair fluttered against her cheek. With one gloved finger, he flicked the hair back into place.

On her back, with her arms and legs straight, she looked like one of those mannequins in the store—not that he was a poser. He didn't need to pose his victims in grotesque and disrespectful positions, but now Kelsey looked as perfect and untouchable in death as she'd looked alive.

He twisted his head over his shoulder and peered into the darkness, swallowing against his dry throat. He'd done his research and this part of the park didn't have cameras, but you never knew who could be watching.

He jumped back and surveyed his handiwork, a flicker of lust stirring in his belly. He'd wanted to have sex with her, but he didn't want to leave his DNA. He didn't want to get caught. He had many more dates in mind. Besides, Kelsey was a nice girl. He could go pick up a hooker on Hollywood Boulevard to satisfy his needs, just as he'd done after his dates with Shelby and Marissa.

Two more steps—the most important ones. He pulled a playing card from his back pocket, leaned over Kelsey's body and stuck it between her lips—the queen of hearts. Then he dug into the front pocket of his jeans and withdrew the box cutter. He knelt beside Kelsey and sliced off the pinkie finger of her left hand.

The souvenir.

Chapter One

"Good thing she was already dead when he took her finger." Detective Jake McAllister lifted the victim's wrist and grimaced. He called over his shoulder, "Tire tracks at the trailhead? We know this isn't the kill site."

"Too many to identify just one." His partner, Billy Crouch, impressive in a dark gray tailored suit, purple pocket square and wing tips, strode down the trail to join Jake where he crouched beside the body. "No tire tracks, no cameras. I had one of the officers check with the park rangers."

"No cameras at the other dump site, either. He's being careful." Jake rose to his feet, inhaling the scent of pine from the trees and locking eyes with an ambitious squirrel who'd been busy scurrying up and down the large oak that provided a canopy over the body.

Griffith Park was an oasis of rugged, untamed land in the middle of the urban sprawl of LA. It housed the zoo, the observatory, a concert venue, a carousel, pony rides and acres of wilderness crisscrossed with hiking trails. It had also hosted several dead bodies in its day, including the Hillside Strangler's first victim.

Jake pointed at the card inserted between the victim's lips. "Queen of hearts, missing finger—looks like we have a pattern here."

Billy whistled as he pushed his sunglasses to the end of his nose. "It's The Player all over again."

"Copycat." Jake raised his hand to the crime scene investigators who had just arrived at the park and waved. "The Player was working twenty years ago and abruptly stopped. He's gotta be dead or in prison."

"Maybe he just got paroled." Billy picked an imaginary speck of lint from the arm of his jacket. "He could've been twenty when he was operating before, spent twenty years behind bars for armed robbery, assault, rape. Now he's forty, tanned, ready and rested."

"Could be. They never got his DNA back then. Never left any—just like these two murders."

Billy whipped the handkerchief, which Jake had believed was just for show, out of his front pocket and dashed it across the shiny tip of one of his shoes. "Damn, it's dirty out here."

Jake rolled his eyes. "It's the great outdoors. Most people don't take hikes in Italian suits and shoes."

Shaking his head, Billy clicked his tongue. "Only the shoes are Italian, man. The suit's from England."

"Excuse me, Cool Breeze." Jake bowed to his partner. He'd given Billy the nickname Cool Breeze, and it had stuck. The man knew his fashion, his fine wines and his women.

Jake had warned him about the women because Billy already had a fine woman, Simone, at home. They needed only one divorce in the partnership, and

Jake had that covered—not that he had run around on his wife, unless you counted the job as the other woman...and a lot of cops' wives did.

Someone cleared his throat behind him. "Fingerprints?"

Jake jerked his head toward Clive Stewart, their fingerprint guy in Forensics, his shaved head already sporting a sheen. "Yeah, you can check, Clive. He didn't leave the knife or box cutter behind that he used to slice off the finger. You might try the playing card, her neck. You know your job, man. I'll let you and the others do it."

As CSI got to work, Jake shuffled away from the body on the ground and eyed the crunch of people beyond the yellow crime scene tape. Although still morning, the air possessed that quiet, suffocating feel that heralded a heat wave, and the tape hung limply, already conceding defeat.

Jake pulled out his phone. Holding it up, he snapped some pictures of the looky-loos leaning in, hoping to catch a glimpse of...what? What did they hope to see? Did they want to ogle the lifeless body of this poor woman dumped on the ground?

Maybe one of them was already familiar with the position of the victim. Killers had been known to return to the scene of the crime and relive the thrill.

He swung his phone to the right to take a few more pictures from the other side of the trail. As he tipped up his sunglasses and peered into the viewfinder to zero in on his subjects, he swore under his breath.

What the hell was *she* doing here?

Billy stepped into his line of fire. "He wanted someone to discover her quickly. She's not that far off the trail, but no purse or ID, so he doesn't want us to identify her right away."

"You're blocking my view." Jake nudged Billy's shoulder and framed the crowd at the edge of the tape again…but she was gone.

Jake took a few more pictures, and then cranked his head from side to side looking for that unmistakable flash of blond hair, surprised she hadn't ducked under the tape by now to nose around.

"Trying to find the killer?" Billy raised an eyebrow.

"Could be watching right now."

"The Player never did that."

"Not that they know of. Would be interesting to see some photos of those crime scenes from twenty years ago."

"I'm sure that's in our near future." Billy patted the top of his short Afro. "Two murders, same MO, both bodies found in our jurisdiction, copycat of a previous serial killer—I smell a task force."

Jake's phone buzzed in his hand, and he glanced at the text from Captain Castillo. "You're downright clairvoyant, Cool Breeze. Castillo wants everyone in Robbery-Homicide at the station at four o'clock. He wants me there at three thirty."

"Uh-oh. Hope you weren't planning on getting a life for the next several months."

"Getting a life? I have a life." Jake dropped the

phone into the pocket of his non-English suit jacket and turned away from the body.

Billy gave a short laugh behind him. "If you say so, J-Mac."

AT 3:28 P.M., JAKE propped up the wall outside Captain Castillo's office in the Northeast Division with one shoulder. Castillo hated tardiness almost as much as he hated the press.

Jake hadn't bothered knocking on the office door because he could hear Castillo's voice on the other side. He'd end the phone call at precisely three thirty and open that door, expecting Jake to be standing right where he was. And if he weren't there? He didn't know. He'd never tempted fate like that. He had to play by certain rules so that he could break others.

The low drone of Castillo's voice stopped, and Jake stood at attention.

The door swung open, framing Castillo, navy suit slightly rumpled, salt-and-pepper hair already escaping from the pomade Castillo slathered on his head. The captain nodded once. "McAllister."

Jake followed the captain into the room, taking the lone chair on the other side of the functional desk, and dove right in. "I'm assuming this is about the two murders."

"It is. We've identified the second victim, Kelsey Lindquist." Castillo shoved a picture of a pretty blonde across his desk. "No connection to Marissa Perez that we can see. They didn't know each other, live in the same neighborhood, work together or in the same industry."

"That's first glance. They're not working girls, so how is he finding them? Marissa did some online dating. Do we have Kelsey's phone?" Jake glanced at the thick file on Castillo's desk. "Looks like Billy's been doing some work while I was in court. How'd you ID the latest victim so quickly?"

"Parents, unfortunately. Kelsey missed work today. Her boyfriend located Kelsey's car in the parking lot of a shopping center this afternoon, purse and phone on the floor of the car. He called the police. The officers took one look at her driver's license and called us."

"Boyfriend?"

"Not a suspect…yet."

"Tough." Jake's gut rolled. If anything ever happened to Fiona, he'd be ready to do murder himself. "Have her parents identified the body?"

"Not yet." Castillo shoved the folder toward Jake. "This is yours now. We're forming a task force, and I want you to lead it for us."

"For us?" Jake drummed his fingers on top of the file. "You expect more bodies in other jurisdictions?"

"You and I both know that's a possibility. He's gotten away with this twice. Do you really think he's going to stop now?"

"The Player did."

"The Player stopped after six." Castillo mopped his brow with a tissue he'd plucked from a box on his desk. "You've already noticed the similarities."

"Copycat."

Castillo shrugged, his suit crumpling even more around his shoulders. He needed Billy's tailor—they all needed Billy's tailor.

"Most likely. Would be rare for The Player to come out of retirement." Castillo steepled his fingers. "I know you're already thinking about The Player's murder book."

"Thinking about the murder book and Quinn. Does he still live in Venice, near the beach?"

"Ned Verona would know for sure. Hit him up after the meeting." Castillo splayed his hands on the desk, thumbs touching. "I'll take everyone through the slideshow of what we have now on both murders. You and Crouch can chime in whenever you feel the urge. Then I'm going to turn the show over to you for an intro to the task force."

Jake slid the file folder from Castillo's desk and tucked it under his arm. Resisting the urge to flip through the pages, he followed the captain into the conference room, already packed with Robbery-Homicide detectives, several uniformed officers and a few civilians.

The lights dimmed, and for the next hour Castillo briefed them on the two murders. Jake picked up where the captain left off, discussing the formation of the task force and how it would operate.

Blinking his eyes as the lights went up, Jake asked, "Any questions?"

Someone yelled from the back of the room. "Are we gonna call this task force The Player 2.0?"

"Not unless you want to send the public into panic

mode. Maybe we'll have a contest. Winner gets extra duty." As the officers and detectives peppered him with questions, Jake scanned the room, his gaze tripping over the blonde in the back.

Oh, hell, no. Had Castillo invited her?

She'd noticed his attention and had taken a step back, folding her arms over a snowy-white blouse, a half smile curling her lip, exuding a confidence born of being connected.

Jake rushed through the rest of the questions, and as the meeting adjourned he elbowed his way toward Castillo, who was talking to Lieutenant Alicia Fields. He waited until Alicia took a breath before butting in. "I need to talk to you, Captain."

Alicia held up her finger. "Do you mind, J-Mac? Give me a minute."

Someone tugged on his sleeve and he jerked his head over his shoulder, meeting the amused blue eyes of Kyra Chase, the quack.

"Get used to it, McAllister. I'm part of this task force—whether you like it or not."

Chapter Two

He didn't like it—not at all.

His hazel eyes narrowed and his nostrils flared, as if he'd just gotten juiced up with adrenaline and was debating between fight and flight. As if Jake McAllister would ever flee from conflict. Quite the contrary. He had a reputation for courting it.

Castillo sliced his hand in the air to cut the tension vibrating between her and Jake. "McAllister, you know Kyra Chase, right? She did a great job on Verona's case a few months ago. Put the department in a good light by assisting with the victims in those gang retaliation shootings, got some cooperation from family members we never expected."

"I know *of* her." Jake thrust out his hand in an aggressive gesture. "Detective Jake McAllister, Ms. Chase."

She clasped his hand, and its warmth and strength rattled her even more than the gesture itself…and the fire in those eyes that had just turned green. "You can call me Kyra. Captain Castillo has assigned me to your task force as a liaison between the victims' families and the investigation."

"You won't be doing any profiling of the killer or coddling any suspects we bring in?" He released her hand abruptly.

She tilted her chin in a challenge. She knew her meeting with McAllister would be adversarial—she just didn't realize how much she would enjoy it. "That's not my job and never has been."

"It shouldn't have been your colleague's job, either."

Castillo cleared his throat. "The Lindquists are going to the morgue tomorrow to identify their daughter. I want both of you there...and civil."

Jake rolled his shoulders. "I'm always civil."

Lieutenant Fields, who'd been quiet through the exchange, snorted and patted Kyra's back. "If you want any tips on how to deal with the ogre, let me know."

Kyra let her eyes wander the length of Jake's fit frame. She'd dealt with worse. "I know you're a top-notch detective, and I look forward to working with you."

She could lie with the best of them, but those two statements were nothing but the truth. Of course, she'd be looking forward to working with Jack the Ripper for a chance to get on this task force.

Jake nodded once. "I'll get your number from the captain, so we can organize for tomorrow."

"I'll be ready." She took her leave of Captain Castillo and Lieutenant Fields and strode from the conference room, which had mostly cleared. Although she could feel McAllister's gaze following her, it would be foolish to turn and acknowledge it, acknowledge him.

She didn't like him any more than he liked her, but she'd face a blazing inferno to stay on this case—and that's exactly what Jake McAllister might prove to be. She'd just have to avoid getting burned.

AFTER SITTING IN traffic for two hours, Kyra poured herself a glass of chilled chardonnay and curled up on her couch with a file folder in her lap. Some people settled in with a good book. She preferred files on murder cases.

She took a sip of wine, the crisp, fruity flavor sliding down the back of her throat and creating a warm spot in her belly. Sometimes she needed something stronger to get through this stuff, but a glass of wine on an empty stomach would suffice for tonight.

She flipped open the folder and shuffled through her notes. She didn't have anything official from the LAPD yet, but she'd get her hands on everything despite Jake McAllister. She understood his distaste for her wasn't personal. She didn't even blame him, but he should do a better job of reining in his emotions. If he wanted lessons, she could oblige.

She ran a finger down a page of notes, pausing at each bullet point where her pen had dug a small hole next to a fact she knew about the two murders. The police hadn't yet released certain details about the homicides, but at the task force presentation Castillo and McAllister had confirmed what she'd already heard— the killer had stuck a playing card between the lips of each of his victims and had removed her left pinky finger.

Kyra flicked her thumb against her own pinky finger and clamped down on a shiver that threatened to rampage through her body. She took another sip of wine, savoring it before swallowing.

The task force would probably reveal one of the killer's proclivities and keep the other one close to the vest to weed out the fakes, frauds and wannabes. Twenty years ago, Roger Quinn had disclosed the card, which was how The Player had gotten his name, but the public never knew about the severed fingers.

That didn't mean the information never got out. People talked.

Had this killer heard the stories? Was he anxious to pick up where The Player had left off? There were cold cases in the annals of the LAPD, but not many serial killer cold cases. Usually, murderers got sloppy or arrogant or desperate for the recognition they felt was their due. But not The Player. She had no doubt he was arrogant, though he'd never been sloppy and he'd never contacted the press or the police to crow about his achievements.

She slid the folder from her lap and rose from the couch, holding her wine in front of her. She placed the glass on the kitchen table and ducked into her bedroom. She swung open the door to her walk-in closet, a rarity in these older, rent-controlled apartment buildings in Santa Monica, and shoved aside some blouses hanging on a lower rod, not doing a great job of hiding her safe. She tapped in the code, her mother's birth date, and waited for the green light to flash its welcome.

She pushed aside her passport, birth certificate and the release papers from LA's foster care system and curled her fingers around the soft, worn edges of a manila envelope. The sharp stub of the clasp, long since broken off, scratched her finger as she slid the envelope from the safe.

Leaving the door of the safe open, she backed out of the closet, clutching the packet to her chest. She swung by the kitchen table on her way back to the couch and grabbed her wine.

Tucking one leg beneath her, she slipped the paper clip, which had taken the place of the clasp, from the top of the envelope and plunged a slightly shaky hand inside.

The sheaf of papers waiting for her fit comfortably in her grip, and she brought them into the light. These weren't official documents, but they told the whole story of The Player's killing spree twenty years ago.

Six women. Six severed fingers. No connection between the victims, except for an age range in their twenties and a general appearance of long blond hair. Nothing unusual in that, hardly a pattern. Young women were more apt to be the target of serial killers, and most young women, then and now, wore their hair long.

The two current women didn't even match The Player's victims, as Marissa was a dark-haired Latina.

Kyra flipped over the stack of papers and slapped

them down on the coffee table. She didn't need to look at the pictures again.

She rolled her wineglass between her hands and raised it to her lips. She'd better slow down and get some food in her stomach if she hoped to carry out her plan tonight.

She pushed up from the couch, poured the wine into the sink and grabbed a container of leftover pasta from the fridge. She ate it cold, standing up, one bare foot on top of the other.

Then she changed from the slacks and blouse she'd worn to work and pulled on some jeans, a T-shirt and a hoodie. When she finished tying her running shoes, she reached into her satchel and grabbed her .22. It wasn't easy to get a conceal-carry permit these days, but she had connections.

She slung the strap of her purse across her body and secured her gun in the outside pouch. She closed the safe in the closet and locked up the apartment, its location on the first floor making it vulnerable to break-ins by petty thieves and junkies, but they didn't scare her. She'd faced the devil himself—more than once. Then she hopped in her car, which was parked in the carport in the alley, and drove back the way she'd come earlier.

It didn't take two hours this time. Rush-hour traffic had thinned out, but the freeway still boasted enough cars to keep her speed below fifty most of the way.

She took the turnoff for Griffith Park, leaving the other cars behind. She crawled down a road toward the trailhead where there'd been a mass of vehicles and people this morning. Now she had the place to herself—she hoped.

This morning, she'd headed to the crime scene as soon as she'd heard a hiker had found a body, the second in two weeks, dumped in the rugged area that nestled in the heart of LA. She'd seen McAllister there, large and in charge, and he'd seen her. He'd been taking pictures of the onlookers, hoping to catch a killer with his camera.

She'd been surveying the crowd herself, but nobody stuck out to her. McAllister's pictures could be valuable further into the investigation once they tracked the movements and acquaintances of these women.

It would've been easier for her if Verona had been tagged to lead the task force, but McAllister was the hotshot, despite certain issues with the department. She could wrap Verona around her little finger, and she could handle McAllister, too. She'd had lots of practice getting the jump on men who thought they ruled the world.

She held her breath as she neared the trailhead. She didn't need some patrol officer assigned to protect the crime scene asking her questions. Her late-night visit would surely get back to McAllister, and she didn't need that, either.

As the car slowed to a stop, she huffed out a breath. She had free rein without an audience. The cops and CSI had been working the crime scene since this morning. They must've squeezed it dry. No need to keep anyone away now.

Darkness met her as she scrambled from her car,

her hand firmly on the zippered pouch concealing her weapon. She didn't expect the killer to be active two nights in a row or choose the same dump site, but this guy wasn't the only evil that lurked in the shadows. She had plenty of experience with evil, and the only way to stop it in its tracks was with a well-placed bullet.

The soles of her running shoes crunched the dried-out discards from the foliage that bordered the trail. A slight warm breeze feathered through the trees, sending another few leaves floating to the ground and lifting the ends of her hair. As summer wound down, it ushered in wildfire season and the debris beneath her feet would be its hapless fuel.

She took several steps down the trail, her breathing shallow, her heart hammering in her chest. He must've parked in just about the same place as she did, his feet treading the same path as hers.

The police had noted drag marks on the trail. Of course, he hadn't killed Kelsey here. He'd brought her to this place, left her, dumped her. Kyra's hands curled at her sides as a hot rage thrummed through her veins.

The wind picked up and whispered down the trail. She whispered a response. "Is it you? Have you come back? If you have, I'm not going to let you get away this time. I'll kill you myself."

A twig snapped behind her and she spun around, her hand plunging into her purse for her gun. A hulking figure took shape under the crescent moon, and she aimed her weapon at it—center mass.

"Take one more step, and I'll drop you where you stand."

Chapter Three

He'd recognize that voice anywhere, even though he'd heard it live and in person just a few times and never so…forceful. He believed her, but he had no intention of letting her off the hook so easily.

He raised his hands. "I'm LAPD Detective Jake McAllister. Are you all right?"

A sudden gust of wind carried her sigh down the trail toward him.

"I—it's Kyra Chase. I'm sorry. I'm putting away my weapon."

Lowering his hands, he said, "Is it okay for me to move now?"

"Of course. I didn't realize, I thought you were…"

"The killer coming back to his dump site?" He flicked on the flashlight in his hand and continued down the trail, his shoes scuffing over dirt and pebbles. "He wouldn't do that—at least not so soon after the kill."

When he got within two feet of her, he skimmed the beam over her body, her dark clothing swallowing up the light until it reached her blond hair. "I didn't mean to scare you, but what are you doing here?"

"Probably the same thing you are." She hung on to the strap of her purse, her hand inches from the gun pocket.

"I'm the lead detective on the case, and I'm doing some follow-up investigation."

"Believe it or not, Detective, I have my own prep work that I like to do before meeting a victim's family. I want to have as much information as possible when talking to them. I'm sure you can understand that."

"Sure, I can. Call me Jake." He pointed to her bag. "What kind of piece do you have?"

"M&P 22 Compact." She clutched the bag with one hand as if she expected him to go for it.

"A Smith & Wesson—nice weapon."

"And before you ask, I do have a permit for it." Her chin jutted forward. "Do you want to see it?"

He raised his eyebrows, even though he'd been planning to ask her about the permit—just to mess with her. "The gun or the permit?"

"Either. Both." She widened her stance.

"I'm good. I've seen the M&P 22 before, and I trust you...about that permit."

"I think I've seen enough." She took a step in his direction and stuttered to a stop, her ponytail swinging over her shoulder, when he didn't make a move.

"Really? You've seen enough? Where's your flashlight?"

She dipped her hand into the pocket of her hoodie

and held up her cell phone. "Phones have flashlights now. They even take pictures."

The corner of his mouth twitched. "Did you discover anything we missed?"

"That's not why I was here." She sniffed. "I have to get going. The Santa Ana winds are kicking up, and my allergies are already giving me trouble."

He stepped aside, and as she walked past him he joined her, matching her stride.

She whipped her head around without slowing her pace. "Where are you going? You just got here."

"I'm going to walk you back to your car because it's dangerous out in the middle of Griffith Park after dark." He pulled up next to her on the narrow trail, bumping her shoulder.

"You forgot I have a loaded pistol as my companion." She patted her purse.

His arm shot out. He grabbed her bag and yanked it quickly to the side. Not only could she not reach her gun, he had the strap of her purse around her neck.

She sputtered, knocking his arm with the heel of her hand. Not a bad response, but her blow made no impact on the grip he had on her purse.

"Just sayin'." He released the bag, and the heavy gun banged against her hip.

"And I'm just sayin' you're an ass." She repositioned her purse, kept her hand over the gun pouch and quickened her pace.

"Having a weapon is better than not having one, but don't let it give you a false sense of security. Just because you're packing heat doesn't mean you can waltz into any situation you please. Have a little common sense."

He followed her stiff back and swinging ponytail back to the road. It was clear she thought he'd been trying to get under her skin, but her appearance here on her own truly alarmed him. He wasn't going to allow Kyra Chase or any other woman to walk back to her car alone under these circumstances. He didn't mind ruffling her feathers.

She hit her remote and her lights flashed once. "This is me. Thanks for the escort, Officer."

His lips twisted into smile. "My pleasure, and thanks for not shooting me back there. I've got your number."

She stopped, her hand on the car door. "What?"

"Your phone number. I got it from Carlos... Captain Castillo. I'll text you the time for our meeting at the coroner's office downtown."

"Right. See you tomorrow." She slammed her car door, cranked on her engine and made a dusty U-turn in the road.

Jake stared after the red taillights until his eyes watered. What the hell had Kyra Chase been doing out here? And who the hell had she been talking to in the darkness?

THE FOLLOWING DAY, Jake parked his sedan in the parking structure of the USC Medical Center downtown. The old building that housed the coroner's office for the county was attached to the med center. He slid from the car and reached into the back seat for his suit jacket.

He'd wait for the comfort of the building's AC before putting it on. The summer in LA had been mild, but September had brought the heat, and the Santa Anas were gusting in the canyons.

He pulled some lip balm from his pocket and swiped it across his dry lips. It couldn't help his dry throat though. Damn, he hated these IDs with the parents. Having Kyra Chase with him might help though he didn't have to like her involvement in any other aspect of the case.

She'd been there that day—the day he'd gone off on Lizbeth Kruger at the station. The day he'd been reprimanded for his behavior. He didn't give a damn—then or now. He'd do it all over again. Even though it hadn't solved anything, hadn't brought back Jacinda, giving Lizbeth a piece of his mind had assuaged his fury. Or at least for that day. His rage had become a living thing inside him, something to tame on some days and something to give vent to on others.

Man, he needed a visit with Fiona.

He strode to the elevator, his suit jacket draped over one arm. He and Kyra planned to meet early near the front door so they could intercept the Lindquists when they arrived for the sad ritual available to the families of homicide victims. Some didn't want or need the last look at their loved one, and in this day of DNA the in-person ID wasn't necessary.

Kyra had to be an old pro at this, although she barely looked older than twenty-five. How'd she manage to look so fresh when hundreds of patients must've poured thousands of sorrows in her ears? Maybe it didn't affect her. Maybe he could learn something from her.

Nah. Therapists were full of it. How do you *feel* about that, Jake? How the hell did they think he felt and how would talking about it change anything?

Not that his old man was a role model, but Jake could understand drowning in the booze. Not the other stuff, but the booze. Hell, he could name ten cops right now who coped that way.

The elevator doors opened and he crossed over to the coroner's office. He slipped into his jacket as he caught sight of Kyra, standing by the door looking cool in her beige skirt and white blouse. She liked white. It made her look…icy.

A smile tugged at his lips as he recalled her clipped tone during their phone conversation earlier today. He'd decided to add the personal touch by calling instead of texting; she hadn't seemed to appreciate his effort.

He'd stung her pride last night when he captured her purse and gun. To be fair, if she were out there on her own and a strange man approached her, she wouldn't let him get that close. Hadn't she drawn down on him when he came traipsing along the trail? Yeah, he'd give her credit for that.

"Good morning." He kept his distance this time, eyeing the leather satchel slung over her shoulder. Did she have her little .22 in there, too?

"Morning." Her blue eyes flicked over him, and he could feel the chill.

He sure hoped she warmed up for victims' families, or she'd be no use to him at all. Verona had sung her praises, but Verona could be wooed by a pretty face and a nice pair of legs. Jake's gaze dropped to the hem of Kyra's knee-length skirt and below. Yep, she had those.

She cleared her throat. "David and Marie should be here any minute. Is the medical examiner ready for us?"

Jake jerked his thumb over his shoulder. "I can check at the desk to make sure."

Jake looked in at the desk where the receptionist assured him the coroner was expecting the Lindquists. The coroner would conduct the autopsy tomorrow. It was always better if the relatives could ID the victim before the autopsy.

As he walked back to Kyra, a middle-aged couple walked through the front doors. Even without an introduction, he knew they were the Lindquists due to their zombie-like appearance. They shuffled into the lobby, the woman with a dazed look on her face and the man drained of all color and life.

Kyra launched forward to greet them, shaking their hands.

By the time Jake joined the group, they seemed like old friends. Kyra turned to him. "Mr. and Mrs. Lindquist, this is Detective Jake McAllister. He's the lead detective on Kelsey's case. Detective McAllister, this is David and Marie Lindquist."

Jake shook David's hand and gave it an extra squeeze just to try to infuse some strength into him. He took a gentler approach with Marie. He cupped her thin hand in both of his. "I'm sorry for your loss."

"C-can we ask you some questions about Kelsey's

death?" Marie's gaze darted to her husband's face and back to Jake's.

Did the two of them have a different approach to how they wanted to handle this? He could understand that. It was a strong marriage that survived the murder of a child.

"I'll tell you what I can, Mrs. Lindquist. There's some information we don't release—even to the family. It gives us a better chance of finding her killer."

"That's what we want." David's watery blue irises were barely distinguishable from the whites of his eyes.

Kyra placed a hand on Marie's arm. "Are you ready? You know, you don't have to do this. You're going to provide her dental records, and that should be enough."

Jake slanted a quick glance at Kyra. Although he knew it would be hard on them, he wanted the Lindquists to ID their daughter this way. They'd have her dental records, her DNA, her picture, but the personal identification seemed to bring some reality to the victims' families, and it also opened up the floodgates sometimes where law enforcement could glean some valuable information for the case. As a victims' rights advocate, Kyra should know this. Maybe she cared more about the families' feelings than catching the killer. In his experience, nailing the bad guy brought peace to the families more than any therapy could.

Marie shook her head. "We need to do this. It wouldn't seem right to let Kelsey take this part of her journey alone. Does that make sense?"

David stared at the dull linoleum floor as if nothing in his life made sense anymore.

Kyra slipped an arm around Marie's shoulders. "It makes perfect sense."

With that settled, at least for Marie, they moved toward the elevator. Jake brought up the rear as he herded the group into the car and stabbed the button for the basement.

In a quiet voice, Kyra asked Marie questions about Kelsey on the ride down.

David murmured to Jake, "Kelsey's murder is connected to that other case two weeks ago?"

"We think so, yeah. We're forming a task force." Jake dipped his head to David's. "We'll get the bastard who did this."

When the elevator settled on the floor, Jake smacked his hand against the door, holding it open for everyone. He'd misjudged Kyra. Marie was hanging on to her like a lifeline, probably confiding things to her about Kelsey she hadn't thought of in years.

That proved it. Kyra Chase was just cold toward him.

They stopped at the door to the morgue, and Jake pressed the button on the outside to announce their presence. A coroner's assistant opened the door, and the chill in the room reached out to grab them. It didn't repel Jake, though. It seemed to suck him inside the room.

"Hello, Detective McAllister, Ms. Chase."

Jake's gaze dropped to the attendant's badge. "Sean, this is Mr. and Mrs. Lindquist."

They had stepped inside, and David looked like he could use Kyra's support even more than Marie could.

Jake had witnessed a few grown men keel over in this space, and he didn't blame them.

At least Sean had taken Kelsey from the drawer. Her body lay covered with a white sheet. They already knew it was Kelsey from the picture on her driver's license left in her car. Her parents had provided a more recent picture, too.

Would he insist on ID'ing the body at the morgue if it were his daughter? Probably, and then he'd insist on fifteen minutes alone with her killer.

Sean cleared his throat. "Are you ready? I'm just going to show her face."

He flicked back the white sheet, and Marie gave a quick gasp.

Jake's eyes swept across the face of the young woman, all life drained from her body. He blinked, for a minute seeing light brown hair and freckles. "Is this your daughter?"

"Yes, that's Kelsey." Marie's voice rang in the room, loud enough to wake the dead in their drawers.

David sniffed and staggered back, his shoulders rounding. The man was going to fold in on himself if Jake didn't get him out of here.

He clasped David's shoulder. "You can leave, Mr. Lindquist."

"Wait." David shrugged off his hand. "That can't be her. That's not my daughter."

Uh-oh. He'd waited too late to get David out of the room. He was having a full meltdown.

Marie sobbed. "What are you talking about, David? That's her. That's our Kelsey."

"Look at her nose, Marie." David thrust out a shaky finger at his daughter's face. "Where's the diamond in her nose?"

Jake's heart bumped in his chest, and his eyes met Kyra's across the body. "Kelsey had a piercing in her nose?"

"They took it out, right? The coroner took it out." Marie grasped her purse strap with both hands.

Jake nodded at Sean, whose red face matched the color of his hair. "We did remove her jewelry and we have that for you, but we didn't remove any diamond from her nose. I didn't even know there was a piercing there. I mean, later…"

Sean trailed off because he meant later, when they did the autopsy, that would be something they would note.

"We didn't notice it at the crime scene, either, Mr. Lindquist. Could she have not worn it that day?"

"She just got it. She wouldn't take it out so soon. She wore it all the time, right, Marie?"

"She did." Marie's bottom lip quivered. "But that's Kelsey, David, with or without the nose piercing."

Jake took two steps toward the door. "Thank you, Sean. Mr. and Mrs. Lindquist, are you ready?"

David stumbled to the door. He'd been ready to leave the moment he'd walked in.

Jake opened the door, and they filed out. The cool air of the hallway felt like a sauna after the morgue, and the stifling air smelled like a spring meadow in comparison to the room they'd just left.

As they reached the elevator, Jake touched David's back. "Are you all right, Mr. Lindquist?"

"I'm okay. I never wanted to do this in the first place. We knew it was her, Marie." David's anger had given him life and color. As he straightened to his full height, he could almost meet Jake nose to nose. "We didn't need to do this."

They piled into the elevator, and Marie sagged against Kyra. As one partner gained strength, the other seemed to lose it. There was only so much strength to go around, and they had to take turns with it.

Jake replied, more comfortable with David's anger than his grief. "I know that was hard, Mr. Lindquist, but we did get some valuable information. Kelsey was not found with a nose stud, so she may have lost it in the struggle with her killer or..."

Kyra hit the elevator button with her fist. "Or he took it."

Chapter Four

Jake watched through narrowed eyes as Kyra handed her card to Marie and stepped away from the Lindquists' car with a wave. Jake lifted his own hand, his heart still sore at their grief.

Kyra spun around on the toes of her low-heeled pumps like a ballerina and strode toward him like a boss, her blond ponytail bobbing behind her. She positioned herself in front of him, arms folded over her white blouse.

"Are you going to order another search of the dump site for Kelsey's nose stud?"

"Of course, but as you noticed last night while you were tromping all over the area, the tape is gone and if the diamond was there it might be ground into the dirt by now. We'll also comb her car for it. If there was a struggle outside or inside her car, it might turn up in the vehicle. She was most likely taken at her car, as her purse and phone were still there."

"And if he took it as a trophy?"

Jake scratched his chin. "Definitely would be unusual for a serial killer to claim two trophies—the finger and the nose stud. Not unheard-of, I guess."

"What about Marissa? Was she missing any jewelry?" Kyra hunched her shoulders as if she'd gotten a sudden chill despite the dry heat blanketing them.

Jake loosened his shirt collar. "Not that we know of. Have you talked to Marissa's family, yet?"

"As they're out of state, I haven't contacted them. I plan to meet with her friends, if they request it."

"We'll check with her friends in LA about the jewelry." A bead of sweat crept down Jake's neck and found a path beneath his shirt, looped tight by his tie. How did Kyra manage to look so cool in her crisp blouse and light-colored skirt? She'd sloughed off the tan cardigan she'd donned for the AC in the building and the even colder air in the morgue. His own suit felt like a straitjacket, constricting and smothering him.

Kyra's gaze dipped to his chest, as if following the trickle of sweat making its way to his belly. "Santa Ana winds kicking up since yesterday. Hope that doesn't mean the start of fire season."

He must look as miserably hot as he felt. "Hope not. Keep me posted on anything you find out from Marissa's friends or Kelsey's mom. You established quite a rapport with her in such a short period of time."

"You sound surprised." She smoothed one hand across her already-smooth hair, making him feel more rumpled than ever. "That *is* my job."

What she had with Marie was more than a job to her. Why was she trying to brush it off? Jake cocked his head. "I suppose it is."

Her phone buzzed, and she pulled it from the side pocket of her purse, giving it a quick glance. "You, too?"

He stopped struggling out of his jacket for a second. "Me, too, what?"

She aimed her phone at him. "You keep me posted, too."

She sauntered off while Jake stared after her, yanking on the sleeve of his jacket. He opened his mouth and snapped it shut.

He couldn't very well yell at that swinging ponytail that they had different jobs and he didn't have to inform her of anything if he didn't want to, which wasn't quite true as long as she was on the task force.

He finally struggled out of his jacket and stalked to his car. As long as Castillo said so, Kyra would stay on the task force.

Jake would have to accept it, but he didn't have to like it.

An hour later, back at the station, Jake stopped by Billy's desk, picked up the file on Marissa Perez and shuffled through it while Billy finished a phone call with the dry cleaner.

When he hung up, he said, "Did you do the ID with the Lindquists at the morgue?"

"They ID'd their daughter." Jake wiped the back of his hand across his dry mouth. "They said Kelsey's diamond nose stud is missing. That didn't turn up anywhere, did it?"

Billy sat back in his chair and wedged one expensive shoe on the desk. "No, are you thinking a second trophy? That wouldn't jive with The Player's MO."

"Maybe she lost it in the struggle to subdue her. Did Jenkins and Washington have any luck with cameras in the area where Kelsey's car was found, catching a car coming and going?"

"They're going through some footage now." Billy jerked his thumb over his shoulder. "Do you want to send some people over to Griffith Park and do a search for the nose stud? How about the parking lot where her car was found?"

"Let's do both." Jake waved the file still clutched in his hands in the air. "Nobody mentioned any missing jewelry for Marissa?"

"Not yet." Billy raised his eyebrows. "How'd it go with Kyra Chase, the victims' rights advocate? I heard she met you at the morgue."

"She was there." Jake's mouth tightened. "Have to admit, she was good with the mom, Marie."

Billy whistled through his teeth. "That's high praise from you, brother. Better watch out, she'll want to shrink your head."

"No chance." Jake snorted and smacked Marissa's file on Billy's desk. "I'm going to look at some reports that have come in since yesterday, and then I'm calling Roger Quinn."

"Going old-school for this one, huh?"

"He does know more about The Player than any other detective, including the FBI guys."

"Speaking of which, the fibbies are looking at our case." Billy swirled the leftover coffee in his cup from a new coffee house down the street. Station blend wasn't fine enough for his palate.

"Let 'em. They play ball with us, we'll play ball with them." Jake rapped on Billy's desk. "Let's nail this guy and save the FBI the trouble."

After skimming through the reports on Kelsey's car and surrounding area, Jake placed a call to Kelsey's boyfriend to set up an interview. The guy had an iron-clad alibi for the time of Kelsey's abduction and murder, but he'd be able to shed some light on Kelsey's habits, schedules, exes—not that Jake believed this was personal, unless Marissa had the same acquaintances.

Then he pulled an index card from the top drawer of his desk and flicked the corner of it. Castillo had given him Roger Quinn's phone number. Although the retired detective had become even more reclusive than he'd been before the death of his wife a few years ago, if he'd been following the news, he would be expecting Jake's call.

He punched in the number and waited through two rings before voice mail picked up, an impersonal automated message intoning in his ear. At the beep, Jake said, "Detective Quinn, this is Detective Jake McAllister, LAPD Homicide. I'm leading a task force—"

A gruff voice interrupted him on what must've been an answering machine connected to a landline. "I know who you are. You can come by at four o'clock today."

Without waiting for Jake's reply, Quinn rattled off his address in Venice and hung up.

His mouth hanging open, Jake eyed the telephone

receiver until the buzz signaled that the old detective had really just hung up on him. The rumors about Quinn were no exaggeration. Jake would have to bring his A game.

Knowing it would take him at least forty-five minutes to traverse the 405 freeway on the cusp of rush hour, Jake stuck his head in Castillo's office at three o'clock. "I got a summons from Quinn for a meeting at four o'clock."

Castillo glanced at the cell phone on his desk. "Better get going then. You should be fine, J-Mac. Quinn doesn't suffer fools...and you're no fool. In fact, you remind me of a younger Quinn. Should be a good lesson—you could be looking into your future."

With those ominous words ringing in his ears, Jake packed up and hit the road in his police-issued black Crown Vic. He'd shed his suit jacket and tossed it into the back seat.

Now, even with the AC blasting, he pulled his tie over his head, threw it into the back with the jacket and rolled up his sleeves. The news on the radio warned of a small brushfire in the canyons of Malibu, but as Jake peered west over his steering wheel, he let out a sigh. The fire department could contain a small fire as long as the winds subsided.

As he cruised off the freeway onto Lincoln, Jake joined the line of traffic crawling along the busy boulevard. He edged from Santa Monica into Venice and buzzed down his window. He preferred fresh air to AC and gulped in the salty breeze from the Pacific.

As he approached Quinn's walk-street on the canals,

Jake kept an eye out for a parking place, even an illegal one. Police business afforded certain perks.

Who would've thought someone would get the bright idea of recreating the canals of Venice, Italy, on a Southern California beach? Tobacco tycoon Abbot Kinney had been so taken with that Italian town, he'd replicated it on the shores of California and dubbed it "Venice, America."

While the area surrounding the canals of Venice left a lot to be desired in terms of crime, gangs and homelessness, the walk-streets along the water, graced with arching bridges, provided a well-heeled oasis for the homes lining the canals.

Jake knew enough of Roger Quinn to know the retired detective hadn't purchased a million-dollar home on the canals several years ago on his cop's salary—any more than Jake had purchased his home with his cop's salary. Quinn's wife, Charlotte, had been a bestselling author of crime fiction before she passed, no doubt culling ideas from her husband's storied career as a homicide detective.

Jake left his car parked on a red curb and traipsed down Canal, entering a different world as he turned onto one of the walk-streets. He checked the numbers on the houses and loped over a low bridge to the other side of the water.

A smooth jazz instrumental floated out the open window of Quinn's modest house. Newcomers to the area had replaced many of the beach cottages with modern monstrosities that loomed over the canal.

Quinn's house crouched between two of those, daring them to encroach on its space.

Jake parked himself on the porch in front of the red door with a flower box, sporting geraniums to match, and knocked hard. Could the old guy even hear over the noise in there?

The music abruptly ended, and before Jake could absorb the stillness the door swung open. Quinn hung on to the door handle, his body blocking the entrance to his home as he gave Jake the once-over from head to toe.

Damn. Maybe he should've kept his jacket and tie on.

The man had once been as tall as Jake, but age had robbed his bones of their fortitude. His wild gray eyebrows collided over his hawklike nose as he thrust a gnarled hand toward Jake. "Roger Quinn. Everyone calls me Quinn."

What his spine may have lacked in strength, the bones of his large spatulate hands more than made up for. Jake gave as good as he got. Quinn wouldn't be the type of man who'd appreciate coddling because of his age.

"Detective Jake McAllister. You can call me Jake."

One of those eyebrows twitched as if it had a mind of its own. "Not J-Mac?"

"You know how nicknames get around at the department, sir."

"Sir? Just Quinn." He widened the door and stepped away from it, leaving Jake to shut it.

"You like jazz, Jake?" Quinn held up an old album cover with a gleaming sax on it.

"I'm more of a classic rock guy." Jake lifted his shoulders apologetically.

"You can have a look at my collection before you leave." Quinn aimed a sandaled toe at a row of albums on the bottom of a shelf that supported an old turntable setup.

"I'd like that."

"But you didn't come here to talk about an old man's record collection, did you?" Quinn waved Jake toward a love seat as he eased into a recliner that had formed to its owner's body and welcomed him home.

Jake perched on the edge of the love seat. "You've seen the news about the two murders, both bodies dumped in Griffith Park."

"I have." Quinn dropped his chin to his chest. "A playing card between their lips, and their pinky fingers missing."

Jake's pulse jumped. "We didn't release the information about the fingers."

"You wouldn't be here if it weren't for those missing fingers, would you?" Quinn's faded blue eyes sharpened for a second as his nostrils flared. "You think this might be The Player back in action again."

"Do you think that's a possibility, sir... Quinn?" Jake's gaze shifted around the room, searching for the wall of honor that would boast the commendations and plaques and pictures with the various mayors and governors. Instead, he scanned a collection of watercolors that depicted the canals outside Quinn's front door.

"Do I think The Player killed these two young women?" Quinn rubbed a hand, suffering from a slight palsy, across his chin. "That might be the best scenario."

"Sir?" Jake shifted forward in his seat, his knees bumping the rough-hewn coffee table and causing a cup of tea to rattle in its saucer.

Quinn's fingers balled into misshapen fists on his knees. "It's my shame. I never brought him in. I never caught him. It's not enough for me to imagine him dead and gone. I wanted him to end his reign of terror on my terms, not his."

Jake made an involuntary noise in the back of his throat and clenched his teeth. He felt the old detective's rage flow into him. He bathed in it.

Quinn closed his eyes. "You know."

"You wish it were The Player killing these women, but you don't think it is?" Jake cleared his throat. "Why is that? I don't have them with me, but I can bring the files later if you want to have a look at them. Captain Castillo would be more than happy to hand them over to you if you're interested."

"I don't need to look at the files to know it's not The Player operating again on the streets of LA." Quinn's sparse lashes flew open. "Why would he start up again? I always had the theory that he stopped because of all the advancements in law enforcement—DNA primarily, but CCTV, cell phones... You young guys have it easy."

"What about the theory that he's been locked up all this time?"

"Even more reason for him not to come out of re-tirement. If he's been in prison for twenty years it's on a felony, and his DNA will be in CODIS now. He's even more at risk today of getting caught than when he was active."

"So, copycat?"

"Most likely."

"I get the playing card, but you guys kept the finger trophies a secret. How would a random copycat know about the fingers?" Jake hunched forward, his fore-arms on his knees.

"You know how that goes, Jake." Quinn spread his hands. "These things get out, despite our best efforts. You have a task force now, not your first. Cops talk. Their wives talk. The victims' families talk—even when you ask them not to. You can't blame them."

"Anything we should be looking out for?"

"You're asking me? I failed." Quinn picked up the teacup and stared into the brown liquid, looking for answers.

"*That* time, but you never failed before. We still study your cases and methods at the academy."

Quinn laughed, a rusty bark that seemed to startle some birds outside his window. "Are you buttering me up, Jake? I didn't think you were that kind of cop."

Detective Roger Quinn knew what kind of cop he was? "I'm not. I'm stating a fact. If you don't want to help out, that's okay. Hell, if I were in your shoes, I don't know that I'd want to dip my toes back into the muck."

"The muck. That it is."

A knock at the door caused Jake's elbow to slip off his knee, and he cranked his head around. Quinn was supposed to be a recluse. "Do you want me to get that?"

"I can get my own damned door." Quinn used a cane at the side of the chair to push himself up and then left it behind as he took measured steps to the front door.

Jake's body tensed as Quinn opened the door without even asking who was there or looking out the window.

A woman's voice, low and lilting, filtered into the house on a breeze. "Hello, Quinn. I brought food."

As Jake half rose from the love seat, his brain ping-ponging in different directions, Kyra swept into the room, a plastic bag swinging from her fingers.

He growled. "What the hell are you doing here?"

She tripped to a stop, the bag swaying back and forth. "Oh, it's you."

Chapter Five

Kyra pasted a smile on her face, a pleasant mask to conceal her emotions. She'd done it a million times. Why hadn't Quinn warned her he'd be having a visitor...and *this* visitor in particular?

She shot Quinn a look over her shoulder. She couldn't put her finger to her lips, but she could wink—and she did.

Jake jumped to his feet, his gaze darting between her and Quinn, a flush staining his throat. He couldn't blame that on the heat, not in the cool confines of Quinn's house, a breeze from the water stirring the white curtains at the front window.

"Didn't mean to overreact." Jake coughed. "You surprised me. I didn't realize you knew Detective Quinn."

Quinn erupted into that hacking laugh of his and slammed the door. "Face it, Jake. You thought Kyra had followed you over here to horn in on your territory."

"I was worried you'd think the two of us were trying to ambush you or something." Jake shrugged.

"The hell you were." Quinn patted Kyra on the back

and nudged the bag with his knee. "Smells like fish and chips from the pub."

"It is." Kyra lifted the plastic bag. "I didn't know you had company or I would've picked up another order."

"That's okay. I was just leaving. We were finished." Jake skirted around the love seat and planted his shoes on the wood floor in a wide stance.

"No, we weren't. I know you had more questions, and since Kyra's on your task force there's no reason we can't discuss this together." Quinn snatched the bag of food from her hand. "Besides, that place always gives you way more fish and chips than you can eat. We'll share."

Jake narrowed his eyes as they shifted between her and Quinn. He obviously suspected a setup. "How'd you know Kyra was on the task force?"

"I still have my sources, J-Mac." Quinn raised a finger, his lips twitching.

Kyra curled her hand around the loop of the bag. "Oh, no, you don't. Sit down, and I'll get you a plate of food."

"Only if you grab a couple of those IPAs in the fridge."

"Did Dr. Wong okay you for beer?"

"I don't need Dr. Wong's approval to live my life." Quinn relinquished his hold on the plastic bag and sank into his recliner. "Jake can help you."

To her surprise, Jake joined her in Quinn's small kitchen, his large presence dwarfing everything even more. She'd figured two strong, obstinate personalities like Jake's and Quinn's would butt heads; instead, Jake showed a gentle deference to the older man that granted him a few more notches in her estimation of him.

She grabbed three plates from the cupboard as Jake reached into the bag for the containers of food.

He turned from the counter, and she almost plowed into him with the plates. She clutched them to her chest. "It's a little crowded in here."

Jake folded his arms, wedging his fists into his bunching biceps. He'd lost the tie, and a dusting of dark hair peeked from the V of his open shirt collar. "How do you know Detective Quinn?"

Kyra swallowed before loudly clanking the plates on the tile counter that divided the kitchen from the living room. Quinn needed to hear this, too. "Quinn and I go way back. I helped out on one of his cases—just like I'm helping you. Isn't that right, Quinn?"

"That's right." Quinn twisted his head to the side. "One of my cases. Kyra's a sharp cookie, and she's compassionate. She adds a lot of value to a task force like this."

"I saw her in action today with the Lindquists." Jake popped the lid from one of the containers of fish and chips, and the aroma of fresh cod filled the kitchen. "Seems like she's a natural."

Kyra almost dropped the forks. A compliment from Jake McAllister? "I was able to help Marie. David's still in too much shock to take in anything right now."

"Two each?" The tines of Jake's fork hovered over a piece of fish. "I can do with one. I don't want to ruin your dinner party."

"It wasn't a dinner party. Sometimes I show up on

Quinn's doorstep bearing food. If he's home and hungry, we'll eat together. If not, I leave it for him." Kyra sealed her lips and dumped some coleslaw on an empty plate. She was giving Jake the impression that she and Quinn had a deeper relationship than a working one. They did, but Jake didn't need to know about it, and Quinn was playing along.

With a frown between his eyebrows, Jake speared a piece of fish and plopped it on the plate next to the coleslaw. "You're a good coworker."

"What's taking you two so long?" Quinn drove his cane into the floor and rose to his feet a little unsteadily. "A man could starve while you stand in there blabbing. And where's my beer?"

Kyra rolled her eyes at Jake. "Kind of demanding, isn't he?"

"Last time I checked, this was my house and you were the intruders." Quinn bellied up to the counter and rapped his knuckles on it. "Beer, no glass, and make sure you drizzle some of that malt vinegar on my fish."

"Yes, sir." Kyra arranged the last of the coleslaw, split three ways, on the plates and spun toward the fridge to grab the beers. Cranking her head over her shoulder, she asked, "Do you want a beer, Jake?"

"I'll take one, thanks."

She held one bottle out to him. "Twist off the cap and give this one to Quinn so he'll take a seat and get out of our hair."

Jake took off the cap with a crack and shoved the

beer across the counter to Quinn. "Take a seat, sir. We'll bring your food out to you."

Quinn grabbed the bottle by the neck and walked back to his chair with a little more spring in his step.

Kyra handed a second bottle to Jake. "I'll take his plate out."

From the to-go cup, she poured a line of vinegar up and down Quinn's fish and spooned some tartar sauce on the plate. "I've got you covered, Quinn."

Two minutes later, they were sitting around Quinn's coffee table, plates of food in their laps and beers in their hands.

"I'm proposing a toast." Quinn raised his bottle. "Let's get the SOB this time."

Jake lowered the bottle from his lips, which were still puckered. "This time? Didn't you just tell me you didn't believe The Player was responsible for these murders?"

Quinn took a long pull from his bottle. When he lowered it, his misty blue eyes had sharpened—either from the booze or the subject matter. "I meant in general. We always want to nail them, and we usually do."

Kyra twirled her fork in the coleslaw. "Don't you agree with Quinn, Jake? At the task force meeting, you didn't seem to put much stock in the theory that The Player had come back online."

"Yeah, I'm leaning that way." Jake picked up a piece of battered fish with his fingers and dredged it in the mound of tartar sauce on his plate. "It's the missing finger that gets me."

"Don't dwell on that, Jake. You and I both know that

stuff gets out, whether we want it to or not." Quinn spread out a piece of paper towel on his lap.

"A lot of times it's leaked from law enforcement." Jake picked up his beer and ran a fingernail through the damp label. "Did you ever suspect a cop as The Player?"

Quinn dropped his fork and it pinged against his plate, flicking a strand of cabbage onto their makeshift dining table. "That's quite a charge."

Jake's gaze shifted to Kyra's face, and then he tipped some beer down his throat. "Not one I make lightly, but it must've crossed your mind. Think about it. If this guy stopped the killing twenty years ago because of advances in law enforcement, he must've been well versed in those advances."

"Or he made it his business to know. The Player wasn't a stupid or clumsy man." Quinn dabbed at the rogue shred of cabbage on the coffee table with his finger.

"Maybe our current killer knows about the severed fingers because he knows about The Player's cold cases. He's seen the files, knows the evidence." Jake lifted and dropped his shoulders. "Just a thought."

Kyra tilted her head and curled one leg beneath her, which brought her closer to Jake on the love seat—close enough to see the gold flecks in his eyes that gave them their hazel appearance in the sunlight. She took a deep breath and said, "If this guy is law enforcement, he also knows about CCTV, cell phone tracking, DNA. All of that is not stopping him if, in fact, that knowledge was what halted The Player's killing spree."

"Not all sociopaths are as careful as The Player. We still have serial killers, despite technology. Some may not know we can track their movements through their cell phones, some may not know which bodily fluids contain DNA, some may not be aware of cameras." Quinn waved a French fry at her. "Some don't care."

A little chill zipped up her spine, and Kyra gritted her teeth. None of them cared. They were driven by some evil inside them. They couldn't be human. Too bad their outer appearance didn't reflect their inner demons for everyone to see and avoid.

"Are you all right?" Jake pointed at her untouched food. "You probably didn't come to visit Quinn to talk about this case. Sorry I ruined your dinner."

Kyra glanced at Quinn from beneath her lashes. "Don't worry about me. This is my work, too."

Jake's lips twisted into a smile, and a flash of heat claimed Kyra's body. That bone he'd thrown her before about her rapport with the Lindquists had been designed to get Quinn on his side. Jake needed Quinn. He didn't think he needed her or her skills at all. He had no idea.

"Jake's right. Eat your food." Quinn wiped his napkin across his face. "You never did tell me what brought you over here, Kyra. To what do I owe the pleasure of your company and fish and chips from the King's Head?"

She dug into her food. "Just wanted to make sure you were taking care of yourself. You know how the air quality aggravates your breathing, and there's a fire near Malibu Canyon."

"Has that been getting worse?" Jake crumpled his napkin and tossed it onto his empty plate. Easing back, he rested his ankle on his knee, extending his arms across the back of the love seat, his hand dipping toward her shoulder, a little too close for comfort. "When I left work, it sounded like the fire department had that under control."

She shook her head. "The winds have been whipping up in the canyons, and the dry brush from the minimal rainfall last winter is fueling the fire. I could smell it when I got out of the car."

"I sat on my deck earlier today reading and didn't notice it." Quinn lifted his hunched shoulders. "But thanks for checking on me."

Jake slid her a glance from the corner of his eye, still wondering at the relationship between her and Quinn. He wasn't LAPD's hotshot detective and first pick for this task force for nothing.

Toying with the last of the fries on her plate, Kyra said, "I knew Charlotte, Quinn's wife. Uh, we got friendly when she needed a therapist's perspective for a certain character."

"I'll have to pick up one of her books. I'm sure your wife must've gotten a lot of ideas from you, sir." Jake hunched forward and lifted his plate. "Are you finished?"

"I am." She stacked her plate on top of Quinn's and handed them both to Jake.

As Jake carried the dishes to the kitchen, Quinn called after him. "Do you want another beer, Jake?"

"I'm good. I have to drive back to my place in Hollywood. Can I get you another?"

Before Quinn could answer in the affirmative, Kyra held up her hand to him. "Think long and hard about that answer."

"You're a tyrant. Are you channeling Charlotte?" Quinn finished the last sip of his beer. "I guess that's a no for me, Jake."

Jake set the dishes in the sink and rinsed them off. "Should I put these in the dishwasher?"

Kyra raised her eyebrows at his domesticity although she'd heard through the grapevine that he was single. As a bachelor, he'd know his way around a kitchen. She just never imagined Jake McAllister doing anything as pedestrian as the dishes—and the past few days, she'd been imagining Jake McAllister doing a lot of things.

"Yes, dishwasher. Are you done with your beer?" Her hand hovered over his bottle.

"Done."

She picked up the bottle and a few mouthfuls sloshed at the bottom. A lot of cops hit the booze to deal with the stress. Jake must have other outlets…or none at all if she were to believe all the stories about him. If you didn't have a way to cope with the anxiety of the job, it had a nasty habit of building up and exploding.

She reached across the table to collect Quinn's empty. The retired detective had had his own issues with alcohol, but Charlotte had straightened him out.

Quinn encircled her wrist with his arthritic fingers and whispered, "Are you all right?"

She gave him a quick nod and rose with all three

bottles clutched to her chest. She joined Jake in the kitchen, where she got a prime view of his backside in his work slacks as he bent over the dishwasher, putting the plates in the slots on the bottom rack. When he straightened to his full height, he almost backed into her.

"Oops." She held the bottles over her head. "I was just going to put these in the recycling bin."

"I'll do it. You know what they say about too many cooks in the kitchen?" He reached up to take the bottles from her hands, moving close enough so that they almost stood chest to chest.

She blinked as she kept her hold on the bottles. "We're not cooking."

He jerked back and when she released the beer, one bottle fell to the floor where it bounced once.

"What the hell is going on in there? That kitchen is too small for the two of you to be dancing around. If he wants to help, let him help, Kyra. You don't have to control everything."

Jake cracked a smile for a brief second before he picked up the bottle. "Sounds like Quinn knows you well."

"But you don't." She leveled a finger at him and flounced out of the kitchen on shaky legs. She wasn't mad at Jake, or Quinn, for that matter, but when Jake had smiled—even though it had been at her expense—something flickered in her heart and she wanted to stomp it out before Jake took up any more space in her brain.

She sat on the arm of Quinn's chair, no longer willing to share the love seat with Jake. When he returned to the living room, he snagged his shoulder holster from a table near the door.

"I didn't mean to stay so long and disrupt your visit...and eat your food. I'm going to head out."

"I invited you and you're welcome back anytime." As Quinn struggled out of his chair, Kyra jumped off the arm and cupped his elbow to give him a boost.

"You don't have to get up for me." Jake slung one strap of his holster over one shoulder. "I appreciate the offer. I think you can provide us with some valuable insight into this case even if it's not The Player back in action."

"I usher you into my house—" Quinn took a step forward, shrugging off Kyra's hand "—I usher you out of my house. Just don't be like this one, showing up unannounced and uninvited to harass me."

Kyra squeezed Quinn's arm. "You wouldn't have it any other way."

"Thanks for the dinner. I'll pay you back or buy you a lunch at the station sometime."

Jake sure knew how to charm a girl.

She tossed back her ponytail. "Save it. I'm good. I just ask that you keep me in the loop. Use my services. I'm no novice at this, and I'm not going to do an end run behind your back."

Jake's eyebrows shot up to a single lock of dark hair that curled onto his forehead.

Did he really think she didn't know why he didn't trust her? She'd been there.

"Yeah, no problem about that sandwich." He reached past her and shook Quinn's hand. "Sir, good to meet you."

When he stepped onto the porch, Kyra slammed the door after him. "What an insufferable...jerk. Did you hear that comment about the sandwich? He'd rather buy me lunch than keep me informed."

"Oh, I don't know. Sounded like he respected you. Sure seemed to be something between the two of you."

"Something between us?" Her mouth dropped open.

"I don't know." Quinn made a beeline for his chair. "Electricity. Excitement. Something like that. You're not immune to his charms."

"Charms?" Kyra blew out a breath as she got Quinn settled in his recliner. "You've been married too long if you think that man is charming."

Quinn's laugh exploded from his chest in a short burst. "Okay, now sit down and tell me what you really think about these murders. You're sure you're doing all right?"

"I'm fine, fascinated, really." She took the side of the love seat that Jake had occupied earlier, and his scent enveloped her—a spicy smell from his deodorant or body wash, activated by the heat, and a not unpleasant odor that she could only describe as pure masculinity.

"Did Jake mention that the second victim was missing some jewelry? It might be a second trophy, in addition to the finger."

"That would be—"

A pounding on the door stopped Quinn in midsentence.

"Quinn, Kyra, it's Jake. I just got some news."

Kyra jumped up, her heart racing, and dashed for the front door. When she swung it open, Jake charged past her, his cell phone in his hand.

"What is it?" Kyra hugged herself, her fingers digging into her arms. "Did they catch him?"

Jake came to an abrupt halt next to Quinn's chair and tapped his cell phone. "Didn't catch him, but he just made a big mistake."

"Someone saw him? He left prints?" Kyra stood at the door, her eyes wide.

"He just called us to give us the location of another body."

Chapter Six

Kyra gasped and brought her hand to her throat. "Another body? That's three now."

Jake took half a step toward her. Likely sensing his movement, Kyra straightened her spine, making it obvious that she didn't play the damsel in distress.

Quinn scratched his chin with the edge of his cane. "Why would he give you this location and not the others? Is it because nobody else found this body?"

"That's part of it. He may have been content to wait, but the fire forced his hand."

Kyra's fingers clawed against the pale skin of her neck. "He's afraid the fire is going to destroy the body and he won't get credit."

"Exactly." Now Jake knew why his first instinct after receiving the call was to return to this room, to these two people who seemed to get it.

"What the hell are you waiting for?" Quinn pounded his cane on the floor. "You two need to get out there."

Kyra brushed past Jake and dropped a kiss on Quinn's cheek. "Take care. We'll keep you posted."

When they stepped outside, Jake's nose twitched at

the faint smell of smoke. "The wind must've shifted. I didn't even smell the fire before."

"Should I follow you over?"

"No point in taking two cars. I have my unmarked vehicle parked on the red. I didn't mean to leave it there that long."

"This is LAPD territory—I'm sure they ran your plate. But if you're offering, I'll tag along with you."

When they made it to the car and slid inside, Jake peeled away from the curb and glanced at Kyra. "I interrupted you and Quinn again."

"Believe me, I appreciated the interruption." She gathered her hair in one hand and dragged it over her shoulder. She loosened it from its regular ponytail, and it shimmered in the dark of the car. "I suppose there's a trace going out on the phone as we speak."

"Yeah, but if it's a burner phone, we'll be out of luck." He accelerated onto the freeway, which had shed half the traffic from rush hour.

She tilted her head at him. "When you walked into Quinn's, you said the killer had made a big mistake. If he used an untraceable phone, how is that a problem for him?"

"Because he made contact." Jake flexed his fingers on the steering wheel. "We have his voice, we have his attention. We know he's following the case. It's not much, but it's more than we had before. Quinn will tell you every piece of information helps."

"Can't hurt, anyway." She tapped on the windshield. "You can see the glow to the west. So, he dumped two bodies in the Griffith Park area and one in Malibu

Carol Ericson   65

Canyon. Do you think this one came before or after Marissa?"

"Probably his first. That's why he dumped Marissa and Kelsey in a more visible area. He realized he concealed his first victim too thoroughly. He must've been climbing the walls waiting for her to be found."

"I wonder if anyone has reported her missing?" Kyra gnawed on her bottom lip.

"We have a lot of missing persons reports come through. Especially here in LA, we don't know if they're really missing or are runaways. Lots of runaways in this city. Lots of people from other places hoping to make it big."

Kyra turned her head and traced her fingers along the glass of her window. "Yeah, city of broken dreams."

After a few minutes of silence, Jake coughed. "Do you live near Quinn in Venice?"

"Close. I live in Santa Monica. That's why I'm able to pop in and see him occasionally."

"So, I'm actually taking you away from your home."

"Where do you live?"

"Hollywood." He kept it short. He didn't want to get into the details of how he lived in the expensive part of Hollywood, in the hills that overlooked the city. He had his street-tough image to protect.

"If it's too much trouble for you to come back this way to drop me off, I can get a rideshare." She finally turned to face him, blinking her eyes rapidly.

He tapped his cheekbone. "Is the smoke bothering you? I can blast the AC."

She sniffed. "The air's fine."

"And I don't mind giving you a lift back to Santa Monica. When there's no traffic, the driving isn't too bad."

"When is there no traffic?" She rolled her eyes. "Just look at it out here. Where are all these people going?"

"I'm sure they all have a story." Jake steered the car off the freeway. "We're probably going to have to show some ID to get close. The firefighters are probably not even allowing residents into the area."

Kyra ducked her head to peer at the orange sky. "Were any structures damaged?"

"Not that I heard, just threatened." Jake slowed down as he hit the twisty roads into the canyon. Gray ash floated through the air and coated his windshield, but he knew better than to smear it across the glass with his wipers.

He squinted at the figure ahead waving his arms. He slipped the badge from his shirt pocket as he powered down the window.

The sheriff's deputy approached the car and bent forward. "What's your business? Residents?"

Jake flashed his badge. "I'm here for the body. Any LAPD on scene, yet?"

"Yeah, couple of patrol officers. They already called the medical examiner's office, but the meat wagon isn't here yet."

Jake grimaced. How did this deputy know whether or not Kyra was a civilian? The cop should watch his lingo, although if Kyra hung out with Quinn she probably knew all about the dark humor.

"Okay, thanks. Let the coroner's van through when

it gets here. I'm not sure how much of the crime scene we're going to be able to process with this fire raging." Jake drove on with the deputy's blessing and pulled behind the LAPD squad car parked on the side of the road.

As soon as he cut the engine, Kyra scrambled from the car and stood with her hands on her hips. "I don't know how much you're going to be able to do here with those flames drawing closer."

He strode around to her side of the car and placed his hands on her shoulders. "You need to wait here."

Her body stiffened, and then she ducked out of his grasp. "I know that. If anyone comes, I'll direct them in. How long do you want to hold off the ME?"

He tilted his head back as a gust of hot wind sent ashes and flecks of cinder swirling around his face. "Not too much longer, or we'll lose the body completely and be running for our own lives. Maybe you should wait in the car."

Jake walked toward the bushes without looking back. He couldn't control Kyra's action. If she wanted to get back in the car, she would. If he hadn't cautioned her against following him to the crime scene, would she have gone with him? Without a doubt.

He almost tripped over the yellow crime scene tape strung between two low bushes. He stepped over it and approached the LAPD officers standing watch over a decaying body, a swath of black hair spread in the dirt.

How did the killer expect anyone to find the body here? Rookie mistake for someone wanting the notice.

He nodded to the officers. "Detective Jake McAllister. Anyone else besides you two?"

"You're the first, sir. We just got orders to book over here and make sure nobody and nothing got to the body."

Snapping on a pair of gloves, Jake crouched beside the young woman and swept a lock of hair from her neck. The mottled color of her skin concealed any strangulation marks; he didn't see any blood or wounds.

Her mouth gaped open but no playing card nestled between her lips. Jake lifted her left hand with its missing finger. The wind must've dislodged the card and carried it away, or an animal got to it.

This looked like a messy first effort. The copycat had improved. Had he made other mistakes with this one? Had he been seen with her? Caught on camera somewhere?

"Damn, we need to get out of here."

Jake sprang to his feet and almost took a swing at Billy. "Why are you creeping around out here looking like a bank robber?"

"Creeping?" Billy tugged on the bandanna covering the lower half of his face. "I called your name, and we both know only white dudes rob banks."

Jake tipped his head toward the body. "Looks like our guy. The card's missing, but so is the finger. I can't tell if it's strangulation, although there are no visible wounds other than animal bites and marks."

Billy rubbed his hands. "And he called us. We

have his voice on tape, even if he used an untrace-able phone."

Jake scanned the blackened hillside. "Tells us something about him that he'd rather risk a call than lose credit for this body."

"Tells us he's not going to stop." Billy jerked his thumb over his shoulder. "Did someone call the victims' rights lady? She's hanging out by the road."

"I, uh… She came over with me." Jake surveyed the ground around the body.

"My man." Billy punched his shoulder. "What's up with that? I thought she was enemy number one."

"This guy is enemy number one." Jake jabbed his finger toward the young woman on the ground. "Kyra Chase is just an…annoyance."

"A good-looking annoyance. Not your usual type—cool, stuck-up, blonde—but worth the exception."

"C'mon, man. I ran into her at Detective Roger Quinn's house. I was there when I got the call about the body, so it made sense to have her tag along. Probably couldn't have stopped her, anyway."

"She knows Detective Quinn? How?"

"Worked a case with him or something."

"She looks great for her age."

Jake whistled. "Hang on, what's this?"

He took two steps toward a bush trembling in the dry furnace and crouched down. He pinched a card between his fingers and rescued it from some of the spiny branches of the bush.

"Not that there was any doubt, but look what I

found?" He held up the playing card to Billy, the queen of spades facing outward.

"Sorry we missed that, Detective."

Jake waved the card at one of the officers. "No worries. You were here to protect the body, not conduct a search."

A firefighter crashed through the bushes and flipped up his mask, his eyes ringed with black soot. "I know it's not the best of circumstances, but you guys are gonna have to get out of here and let the coroner load the body. The winds haven't died down yet, and that fire's going to leap into this area in the next thirty minutes, if not sooner."

Jake tucked the playing card into a plastic baggie. "The coroner's van is here?"

"Yeah, being kept at bay by a bulldog of a woman out there. Is she really with you?"

"She's part of our task force, and I asked her to buy me some time." Jake patted the cell phone in his pocket. "I took pictures and did a search of the area. It has to be good enough."

Jake followed Billy back to the road, which now included a TV van, several more sheriff's deputies and the medical examiner's truck.

His eyes met Kyra's through the glare of the lights and activity, and he dropped his chin to his chest. She nodded back.

He peeled off his glove and shook the coroner's hand. "Same killer. I want to go back in there with you while you move the body so I can take a look underneath."

The reporter shouted over the noise of the helicopters that were now circling in to dump water. "Is this the same killer of Marissa and Kelsey, Detective? Who found the body? Did the firefighters find the body? Did he leave a playing card this time?"

"No comment." Jake tugged on the coroner's sleeve. "We'd better get going. We have less than thirty minutes to get her."

Jake and Billy searched the area some more as the coroner lifted the woman's dead body and zipped her into a bag. Like the other dump sites, this one was clean—no cigarette butts, no gum wrappers, no footprints, no tire tracks. Time and the coroner would tell if the killer had left any fingerprints or DNA on the body.

They needed to identify this woman as soon as possible to start their investigation. If this was the copycat's first victim, he may have made other mistakes—and Jake planned to pounce on every one of them.

He gave the scene one last look before retreating to the road. Flames had started creeping over the ridge, and they'd be racing down the hillside in a matter of minutes.

When he got clear of the trees and bushes, he returned to a calmer scene. The cops and reporters had heeded the advice of the firefighters and fled the area.

Billy waved at him from the front seat of his car. "I'll check in with you tomorrow morning. Hoping for some good news on that phone."

"Me, too." Jake swiveled his head from side to side, his pulse ratcheting up a few notches.

"Oh, yeah." Billy stuck his head out the window as he made a U-turn. "Kyra told me to tell you she got a ride home."

"A ride? With who?"

"That reporter." Billy's fingers formed a gun. "Watch yourself with that one, brother."

Jake swore as he watched Billy's taillights fade into the rolling smoke. Kyra was friendly with reporters, too? That was a bad sign.

He slid into his own car, his tongue sweeping across his lips. Felt like he'd just smoked a pack of cigarettes without a filter.

At least the drive back to his house in the Hollywood Hills was closer than making the trek back and forth to Santa Monica. He cruised downhill and escaped from the canyon that had turned into a hellhole.

When he reached his house and climbed from the car, he sniffed the air. Despite the smell of Hades and the ominous glow to the west, you'd never know there was a fire raging out of control.

Jake undressed, tossed his soot-flecked pants in the corner and stepped into the shower. He let the luke-warm water stream down his back as he scrubbed the grime of the day from his body. He didn't even have to land in the middle of a wildfire to feel dirty. His job left a coat of filth on his skin almost daily.

After his shower, he pulled on a pair of gym shorts and a white T-shirt. He scooped some rocky road ice cream into a bowl and carried it, along with his laptop, to his couch in the living room. He clicked on the TV and watched footage of the fire in Malibu Canyon—no mention of a body yet.

He spooned a hunk of ice cream into his mouth and let the cold sweetness melt down his scorched throat. When he'd finished half the bowl, he muted the TV and logged in to an LAPD database. It didn't take him long to bring up Detective Roger Quinn's homicide cases. One jumped out at him in glaring red typeface—The Player—six unsolved murders. A cold case, the bane of every detective's existence, the stuff of nightmares.

Jake wasn't interested in looking at that case. He had the files and was prepared to study them in more depth. He scrolled down to Quinn's more recent cases, the ones toward the end of his career, the ones where he must've worked with Kyra.

Quinn had wrapped up his last homicide case a few months before he retired, ten years ago. Billy's words at the fire had been niggling at the corners of his mind on the ride home. Billy had said something about Kyra looking great for her age.

Jake didn't know Kyra's age, but she couldn't be older than thirty, could she? Even if she'd worked with Quinn on his last case for the department, that would mean she would've been twenty at the time. What twenty-year-old had a degree in psychology and enough hours under her belt to get assigned to a homicide task force?

He did a quick search of Kyra Chase. One of those people finder sites had her age at twenty-eight, and he discovered she'd gotten a master's degree from Cal State LA in psychology four years ago. That meshed with her age and meant she'd been eighteen years old when Quinn worked his last case for LAPD.

The sweet ice cream on his tongue turned bitter. She'd been lying about how she knew Quinn. Quinn had been lying about how he knew Kyra.

And he was going to find out why.

Chapter Seven

"Thanks for the ride, Megan. I knew you lived in the Marina or I wouldn't have asked." Kyra rubbed at a smudge of ash on her denim skirt.

"No problem, as long as you don't mind the ostentatious ride." Megan Wright patted the dashboard of the news van. "I'm on the job, so I take the van home with me."

"Don't mind a bit. I didn't want to bother the detective for a lift back, and I didn't want to stay in the middle of that inferno any longer than I had to." Kyra took a gulp of water from the bottle Megan had dug out of her cooler in the back. She closed her eyes as it slid down her parched throat.

"Can't give me anything about what McAllister and those cops were doing out there?" Megan flashed her white teeth in her best news reporter smile.

"Wooded area, lead detective on serial killer task force, coroner's van. I'm sure you can figure it out." Kyra put her finger to her lips. "But I'm not giving you anything official."

"You are on the task force, though, aren't you?"

Megan scooted forward in her seat, barely able to see over the steering wheel of the big van.

"I am." Kyra tipped the water bottle at Megan. "And if I'm ever cleared to release any information, you know I'll hit you up first. Now's not the time. We don't want to compromise anything."

"What's he like?"

"Who?" Kyra's heart thumped too loudly in her chest.

"Oh, come on. You know who. J-Mac. He's hot in that brooding kind of way cops have. Just makes you want to get under their skin, and I mean that in every possible way." Megan puckered her lips.

"He's as you would expect—rude, curt, arrogant." Also, gentle and respectful to Quinn and helpful in the kitchen. Kyra lifted her shoulders. "Typical cop."

"Is he married?" Megan lifted one eyebrow in expert fashion.

"No."

"So, you are interested enough to know his marital status."

"Oh, please. I'm around that station a lot. You tend to learn things about people. I think I had heard he's not married."

"Does he have a girlfriend?" Megan lodged the tip of her tongue in the corner of her mouth, as she maneuvered the van around a sharp turn.

Did he? Kyra pressed a hand flat against her stomach. "Does the station realize you don't know how to drive this thing?"

"It's a battering ram, practically indestructible." She

squinted at the road. "Tell me where I'm going. Venice is creepy this time of night."

"You can make a U-turn at the end of the block and then pull over to the right. I'm going to stop in to see my friend first."

Megan slapped both hands against the steering wheel. "You're going to go traipsing around the canals by yourself with a serial killer on the loose?"

"I'm packing heat, girl, I'll be fine. None of the women were from this area or were taken from this area. I have a better chance of tripping over a homeless guy."

"That's no picnic, either." Megan bit her lip as she cranked the wheel for the U-turn. She had to back up and give it another try.

"Neither is being in this van with you." Kyra rapped one knuckle against the window. "Here, here."

Megan rolled to a stop and watched two joggers run past the van. "At least it's not completely deserted."

"It's not deserted at all. It's a warm night. There will be people on the canals, outside their homes. Don't worry about me."

As she reached for the door handle, Megan grabbed her wrist. "You think because you carry that gun, you're invincible. At least text me when you get to your friend's house so I know you made it inside okay."

"I will. Thanks again for the ride and, for heaven's sake, get yourself a pillow to sit on so you can at least see over the steering wheel." Kyra slammed the door and waved to Megan, who stayed idling at the curb until she made it to the bridge that would take her to Quinn's side of the water.

Quinn's neighbors were in their front yard in lawn chairs, drinking beers. Kyra had never officially met them, but she waved anyway and they returned her greeting. Before reaching Quinn's door, she sent a quick text to Megan to assure her she'd reached her destination.

She didn't want Quinn to get out of his chair if he didn't have to so she used her key to open the door and slipped inside his house. The blue light from the TV cast an eerie glow in the dark living room. Quinn often fell asleep in front of the TV.

She tiptoed to his favorite chair, which he'd already abandoned for his bed, and placed her hand against the warm back.

"Kyra, that you? If not, I've got a .45 pointing at the bedroom door."

"Don't shoot." She crept to his bedroom and wedged her shoulder against the doorjamb. "Sorry to show up so late. I thought you might still be up."

"I just hit the sack." He dropped his gun on the nightstand with a clatter. He hadn't been kidding about his .45. "I drank a second beer and it did me in. What did you find out?"

"Not much. McAllister wouldn't let me near the crime scene."

"You can't blame him for that. He's been burned before by a helpful psychologist."

"You *would* stick up for him."

"He's a good cop. Did he tell you anything?"

"We didn't talk, but when he emerged from the bushes I saw it on his face. The call wasn't a hoax. We do have another victim." She folded her arms, shoving her fists under her armpits.

"You didn't talk? You mean he didn't drive you home?" Quinn struggled to sit up against the headboard of his bed.

"Settle down. I took off before he had the chance." She took a step into the room, which still smelled like Charlotte's perfume. "He went back in with the coroner, and the scene was getting too hot to handle—literally. The fire was raging closer and the firefighters advised us to clear out. A friend of mine, a reporter, was there so I asked her for a ride back. She lives in Marina del Rey."

"All right, and you've got your car here." Quinn yawned and tossed back the covers.

"Where do you think you're going?" She loomed over his bed and twitched the blanket back into place.

"I'll walk you out to your car."

"Don't be an idiot. Your neighbors are outside, partying, and you're not the only one who's armed and dangerous." She patted his pillow. "Relax."

As Quinn burrowed his head against the pillow, his tired eyes narrowed to slits. "That gun is not a magic shield."

"I know, but it helps. Get back to sleep." She squeezed his arm under the covers. "We'll talk later."

"You do realize Jake was suspicious about our relationship, don't you?"

She made a half-turn at the bedroom door. "I know that."

"You're going to have to tell him sooner or later, sooner being better. The man has trust issues."

"I know that, too. Let me do this my way, Quinn."

"You always do, Mimi."

Her nose stung as the nickname floated toward her in the dark. She left the bedroom door open, turned off the TV and locked up.

As she stepped onto Quinn's porch, a warm breeze ruffled the ends of her hair and she sniffed the air. The firefighters were still out there doing battle with the forces of nature…and maybe the forces of man.

Had the killer set the fire in the hope that the body would be discovered? To give him an excuse to call it in? She hoisted her purse on her shoulder and huffed out a breath. She'd be giving him credit for the Santa Ana winds if she kept on this path.

He probably wasn't as smart as he thought he was. They never were—except for The Player.

She ground her teeth together and marched toward the bridge. Quinn's neighbors had called it a night. The water lapped against the man-made shores, and the wooden bridge whispered and sighed as she crossed it.

When she reached the other side, she walked at a fast pace toward the street, her head held high, her arms swinging at her sides, her blood pumping. Both Quinn and Megan had her pegged. Ever since she'd gotten her conceal and carry permit, with the help of Quinn, she felt invincible.

Had she been courting danger? She had dismissed that accusation from Quinn. Going about your business didn't count as inviting danger—at least it shouldn't.

A shadowy figure shuffled toward her when she reached the corner, and her hand hovered over the weapon in her purse.

"Spare some change, lady?" The homeless guy peered at her through a curtain of shaggy, sun-bleached hair.

"No, sorry." She marched past him as he called after her.

"God bless you."

Her heart rate returned to normal when she hit the street and a few cars whizzed by. Unlike Jake, she didn't have the perks of a city-issued vehicle and always parked in the public lot when she visited Quinn. The lot still contained several cars. People could be down at the beach or hitting the bars and restaurants on Washington. She was not taking undue risks by walking to her car at night.

The murdered women probably didn't believe they were taking risks, either, but they didn't have a gun— the great equalizer. On the ride home, she checked her rearview mirror often. Just because she had that gun didn't mean she wanted anyone following her to her apartment.

She pulled into her parking spot behind the apartment building and slid out of the car. She held her breath as she walked past the garbage bins and shoved her key into the gate. Management had replaced the swinging wooden door out here with a solid gate with a lock after thieves had targeted several of the units. Hers had escaped, but then she'd secured additional locks on her doors and windows a few years ago.

As she unlocked her front door, the stray cat she occasionally fed rubbed against her ankles. Her neighbors didn't appreciate her efforts on behalf of Spot, but she'd won him a reprieve by convincing them he was keeping the rats away.

"Hope you've been doing your job, Spot. Wait here and I'll give you some milk and food."

He meowed in response, knowing full well his flea-riddled body wasn't welcome inside her apartment.

She'd left a lamp burning earlier, and smacked her purse down on the kitchen table to rustle up some grub for Spot. She shook a little dry cat food into one bowl and filled the other with milk, noticing her full trash can when she threw away the milk carton.

She placed the bowls on the cement outside her front door and returned to the kitchen to grab her trash. When she walked out the door, swinging the plastic bag, Spot flattened his ears against his head.

"Sorry to disturb your dining, Spot." She chuckled. "Dining spot, get it?"

She shoved through the gate, careful not to allow it to clang behind her. The neighbors didn't like that, either. She held open the lid on the dumpster with one hand and swung her trash bag in, letting it fall with a soft squish.

As she turned, something on the ground caught her eye. A piece of trash must've found its way out of the bag. She crouched down and nearly toppled over as the queen of hearts stared back at her from a playing card.

Chapter Eight

Jake's throat felt scratchy from his time in the inferno last night. He'd gargled with mouthwash this morning, which could've been a mistake. He popped his fifth throat lozenge of the day into his mouth and cruised into a conference room being set up for the task force.

Brandon Nguyen, their tech guy, glanced up and tapped on the desk next to him. "This is yours, Detective. Phone and network lines are in, and your computer's already been moved over."

"Thanks, Brandon. Did you account for a few visitors? The body last night was found in LA County Sheriff territory, not our division. Their homicide guys are gonna want to weigh in."

"Captain Castillo already informed me, and we're getting it covered."

"Damn, you're on top of things." Jake crossed the room and hoisted his bag on top of his assigned desk. "Any news on that phone call last night?"

"Our team's on it. We expect something shortly."

Jake pivoted. "Are you telling me that call didn't go right back to a prepaid cell phone?"

"Doesn't look like it, but we'll know for sure within the hour, I'm thinking." Brandon pointed to the desk next to Jake's. "We're putting Detective Crouch's desk next to yours. Is that okay?"

"He has to sit somewhere." Jake winked and pulled up a chair. He flipped open the file from the body last night. No easy ID had been forthcoming. Preliminary info gave them a woman between the ages of eighteen and twenty-five, Caucasian, five foot four inches, approximately 135 pounds, tattoo of a butterfly on her back, no fingerprints on file. He'd assign someone the task of going through missing persons reports to look for a match, if that person could wrestle them away from Billy. Ever since Billy's youngest sister had gone missing, he'd taken a personal interest in the reports.

Other officers had done a search of Kelsey's car and the area around it for her diamond nose stud, and had come up empty so far. Another search of her body's resting place hadn't yielded anything, either.

Had the copycat gotten greedy and taken two souvenirs? It was unusual, though not unheard-of. Better for them, more to tie him to the crimes once they nailed him.

Billy sauntered into the room and perched on the corner of Jake's desk. "How can you work with all this racket going on?"

Jake reached over and tapped the desk next to his. "This is for you, Cool Breeze. I had Brandon over there set you up right next to me so I can keep an eye on you."

"Seems to me you're the one who needs watching.

We were interrupted last night, but I was going to tell you that Kyra Chase is too young to have worked with Quinn on a case. That's not how she knows him, so if that's what she told you—" he lifted his shoulders and his tailored shirt barely creased "—she lied. Thought you had your fill of lying women."

"Yeah, I misunderstood. That's not what she told me. She knew Quinn's wife, the mystery writer, Charlotte Quinn." Jake rubbed his chin, not sure why he'd jumped to Kyra's defense. Maybe it was a mystery he wanted to figure out for himself.

"That makes more sense." Billy rose from the desk and peeled off his suit jacket. "If you continue to hang out with Kyra, see if you can get me an introduction to Megan Wright. Just saw her on the morning news on KTOP and she's fine."

"You're married, Billy." Jake dusted the spot on his desk where his partner had been sitting.

"Technically, but we're separated again. Simone deserves more in a husband, and the kids need more than a part-time dad." Billy's megawatt smile dimmed as he hung his jacket on the back of his chair.

Jake opened his mouth and then snapped it shut. He was in no position to give marital advice. Maybe Billy was right. Simone deserved better than a stressed-out cop using bad behavior to curb his anxiety. Tess sure had.

Brandon bolted from the room, calling over his shoulder. "They got it."

"What's he talking about?" Billy raised his eyebrows.

"The phone call. They traced the phone call." Jake was out of his chair by the time Brandon rushed back into the room, waving a piece of paper.

"I have it, Detective. We got the phone, and it's not a burner."

Jake snapped his fingers. "Let me have it."

Brandon handed the paper to him, and Jake scanned to the pertinent information—the registered owner's name. "Rachel Blackburn?"

Billy leaned over his shoulder. "Could be a wife or a girlfriend."

"This guy hasn't left one fingerprint or one sliver of DNA. Do you really believe he's going to use his wife's cell phone to call in a tip about a body?" Jake pinged the piece of paper with his fingertip.

"Of course not. Hoping for anything on the guy." Billy let out a long breath, and the edge of the paper fluttered. "He got that phone somehow, didn't he?"

"He sure did, Cool Breeze, and we're gonna find out how." Jake held out his fist for a bump from Brandon. "Hey, thanks to your team, Brandon. We give you something to do and you deliver every time."

The kid puffed out his chest a little. "Anything we can do to help. That's why we're here."

Billy asked, "I suppose you tried calling the number again after last night?"

"Same thing as before." Brandon shook his head. "The phone's dead, doesn't even go to voice mail."

Jake rolled up the paper and tapped Billy on the

chest. "We're going to track down this Rachel Black-burn and find out the location of her phone—if she knows."

Fifteen minutes later, Jake had talked to Rachel's mother and gotten Rachel's place of work. Mrs. Black-burn had informed Jake that her daughter lost her phone yesterday. If she wondered why an LAPD detective was interested in her daughter's lost cell phone, she didn't ask.

Billy grabbed his jacket from the back of his chair. "Where does Rachel work?"

"Clothing shop on Melrose." Jake draped his own jacket over his arm and logged out of his computer.

"Right up my alley." Billy laced his fingers and cracked his knuckles.

"A *women's* clothing store."

"It's still on Melrose. Let's go, partner."

As they reached the door, Jake dug into his pocket and tossed the car keys to Billy. "Start the car and get the AC going. I have to ask Brandon something."

He watched Billy cruise down the hallway and turned back into the room. "Brandon, did Captain Castillo ask you to set up a workstation for Kyra Chase? She's our victims' rights advocate."

"Yeah, he did." Brandon leveled his finger at a desk in the corner. "That's for Ms. Chase."

"Has she been here yet? You know who she is, right?"

"Yeah, I know Kyra. She hasn't been around today, but I'll let her know which desk is hers when she shows up." Brandon's brow furrowed. "Do you want her somewhere else? I could move her station to the other side of the room."

"That's all right. Leave it." Jake stalked from the room. His distrust of therapists had even reached the tech department. He'd gotten a handle on his anger after the incident with Lizbeth Kruger when she'd used him and information about a case to get a lighter sentence for a killer, but if something similar happened with Kyra he didn't know if he could trust all his deep breathing exercises to get him through his rage.

As he stepped into the parking lot, Billy cruised forward in the sedan. Jake got in, tossing his jacket in the back seat.

Billy dialed up the AC and pulled away from the station. "Is Rachel expecting us?"

"Her mom said she'd call the shop and let her know. I guess Mrs. Blackburn thinks the LAPD tracks down all lost cell phones because she didn't seem all that curious."

"Really?" Billy slid him a look from the corner of his eye. "The way you come across sometimes, people are afraid to ask questions."

Jake lifted one corner of his mouth into a smile. "That's why I bring you along. You're the good cop, and I'm the very, very bad cop."

They battled the traffic into West Hollywood and nabbed a parking space at a meter a block away from Rachel's store.

They walked to the shop, conspicuous in their suits while dodging hipsters with hats and facial piercings.

Jake let out a breath when he ducked into the cool, dark shop.

The musky scent tinged with roses and lilacs enveloped him, and he gave himself over to its soothing qualities. Aromatherapy always made more sense to him than talking therapy.

A young woman behind the counter glanced up at their entrance, her heavily lined eyes widening. She held up one finger to them and continued talking to her purple-haired customer at the counter.

"Hey, look at this." Billy elbowed him. "They do nipple piercing here."

"Knock yourself out, brother." Jake leaned past Billy to read the sign. "They also do nose piercing. Maybe we found a connection to this shop."

The young woman with the purple hair left the store, and Rachel came from behind the counter, her black Doc Martens clumping on the wood floor. "Are you the detectives my mom called about?"

"Yes, I'm Detective McAllister and this is Detective Crouch. You're Rachel Blackburn?" Jake stuck out his hand, and she grabbed it, the tattoos on her arm marching from her wrist to her shoulder in a colorful sleeve.

"Yes, sir." She gave his hand a firm, professional squeeze and turned to Billy. "Nice to meet you, although I'm not sure why my missing cell phone is cause for the LAPD to pay me a visit."

At least she had more curiosity than her mother. "Is there someplace we can talk privately?"

"Sure." She cupped her hand around her red-lipsticked mouth. "Gustavo, can you come out front for a bit?"

A beaded curtain in the back of the store clacked and stirred, and a young man with a shock of platinum hair growing out of the top of his head like the feathers of some exotic bird emerged. "What do you need, chica?"

"I need to talk to these two detectives in private. Can you handle the customers while I'm busy?"

"I sure can." Gustavo strutted across the floor. "She didn't do it, officers. I can vouch for her."

Rachel rolled her eyes. "Don't mind him. You can follow me."

She sailed through the beaded curtain and held it open for them. Flinging her arm to the side, she said, "This is where we do our piercings, but everything's sterile."

"We're not from the health department." Billy sat on the chair that looked like it belonged in a dentist's office, and Rachel sat on the chair next to his. Jake remained standing.

"I take it you haven't found your cell phone yet?"

"I haven't. It's dead because it doesn't even roll to my voice mail, and when I texted it from my friend's phone, the message wasn't delivered." She hunched forward, brushing wispy black bangs from her eyes. "Why are you interested in my phone?"

"Whoever stole it or found it used your phone to make a call." Jake loosened his tie. "And we're very interested in the person who made that call."

Rachel nodded. "I get it."

Jake had no doubt she did. Despite her punk rock appearance, Rachel struck him as conscientious. "So, if you have any idea where you lost the phone, your last usage, if anyone seemed interested in your phone—that's going to help us find that person."

Billy crossed his ankle over his knee. "We're also getting your phone records, so knowing your last text or call before the phone went missing might help you pinpoint that time."

"I can tell you, it was somewhere on Melrose." She gripped the arms of the chair. "I worked yesterday, almost all day. I got coffee, I got lunch, I stopped in another clothing store where my friend works."

"All on Melrose." Jake had dipped into his pocket for his notebook. He liked taking notes the old-fashioned way, and a lot of people didn't want to be recorded.

"Yes, I can tell you which stores I entered. I must've lost it at one of those places because I had it when I came into work, and I noticed it missing when I left work around three o'clock in the afternoon. I never use my phone at work, so I suppose someone could've stolen it from my bag here." She circled her finger in the air. "As you probably already know, there are a lot of cameras in this area."

Jake and Billy exchanged a look. Rachel was practically doing their job for them.

"Can you tell us the names of the stores and the times?" Jake's pen hovered over his notepad.

"Uncommon Grounds at ten o'clock when I got in." She raised her eyes to the ceiling. "Eat A Pita at around noon for lunch, and another stop at Uncommon Grounds for a frap to get through the rest of my workday, and a quick stop at Jenny's, where my friend works."

"Did you use your phone to make any purchases?"

"No, just my debit card."

Jake tapped his pen against his notebook. "That's really helpful, Rachel. We can scan the CCTV footage near those places, around those times, and see if we can spot anyone in your vicinity."

"Glad I could help. My mom's upset with me because she thinks I was careless with my phone, which my parents pay for, but I've never lost my phone before. I think someone definitely stole it, turned it off so it couldn't be tracked from the time he stole it, and then turned it back on to make the...call. Can you tell me what the call was about?"

"No, I'm sorry. We can't." Billy fished in his pocket and handed her his card as he struggled out of the piercing chair. "Give us a call if you find the phone, or if anything else out of the ordinary happens."

"Out of the ordinary?" The corner of her eye twitched. "Is this person dangerous?"

"I don't think you're in any danger, Rachel." Jake added his card to Billy's. "One more thing. You do nose piercings here?"

"We do."

"Do you keep records?"

"My boss wouldn't have it any other way." She pushed to her feet and pulled back her shoulders. "What do you need?"

Jake shoved his notebook into his pocket. "If we

gave you a time period and a name, could your records tell us if that person got her nose pierced here?"

"I'm sure we could." She dove through the curtain, sending the beads into a frenzy. "Gustavo, I need to look up piercings from…" She twisted her head over her shoulder.

Jake responded. "About two weeks ago, a nose piercing."

"Check the credit card receipts, chica. It's all there." Gustavo folded his hands with his black-painted fingernails on the counter. "Has she been giving you the third degree?"

"I'm afraid it was the other way around." Jake cocked his head. "What do you mean? Rachel's been really helpful."

Gustavo lifted his narrow shoulders and spread his hands. "Rachel wants to be a cop."

"You do?" Jake studied Rachel behind the counter, rummaging through a drawer.

A color the same hue as her lipstick rushed into her cheeks. "Maybe eventually. I have one more semester at Santa Monica College where I've been studying criminal justice before I get my AA degree. I'd like to get my BA under my belt before I think about being a cop."

"What about Dispatch?" Jake rubbed his chin. Dispatch could always use calm, professional, smart people. "I think you'd do great there."

"Really?" Her voice squeaked. "That would be like taking calls?"

"Yeah." He tapped his card, which she'd put on the

glass counter. "Give me a call if you're interested. Seriously, I could get you an interview."

Rachel's dark eyes sparkled as she returned to her task.

Jake asked, "What if she paid cash?"

"The receipt wouldn't be there for cash. We could print those from the register, but they wouldn't tell you anything." Gustavo flicked his fingers in the air. "Nobody pays cash anymore."

Rachel pulled out a stack of receipts between her long fingernails and waved them back and forth. "Okay, two weeks ago. We're looking at the end of August into September for credit card purchases."

"Do those receipts cover those dates?" Jake held out his hand.

Rachel's fingers curled around the receipts, crumpling them at the edges, before she slapped them into his palm. "Yep. Nose is nose piercing and NP is nipple piercing to distinguish them."

Billy hovered over Jake's shoulder. "Do you get a lot of requests for those nipple piercings?"

"Why? You interested?" Rachel's red lips spread into a wide smile.

Jake smacked Billy on the back. "Yeah, you go in the back with Gustavo while I go through these receipts."

"I'm not asking for me." Billy snatched half the receipts from Jake's hand. "I'll look at these."

Jake plucked out all the receipts for nose piercings, checked the dates and looked at the signatures as the receipt didn't have the cardholder's name printed on it.

His pulse jumped as he squinted at a large *K* and a
py *L* at the bottom of one of the receipts for a nose
ing.

lly, I think I got it. I think she came here to get
pierced."

hoisted half her body over the counter to eye
ke held in his hand.

lid back to her side of the counter, she
d against her heart. "Oh, my God.
lquist, one of the copycat's victims.
a killer has my phone?"

ntain-
art, the

nd forth,
get that?
body last
d the queen
sealed away."
ff-the-books.
know if there
he chain of evi-
raise any alarms
d, especially if it

ced it on his palm,
for a man his age.
e was a scholar not a

"Follow me. I can dust
you one." She followed

Chapter Nine

"I need a favor." Kyra dangled the plastic bag c[ ]
ing the queen of hearts in front of Clive Stew[ ]
fingerprint technician.

His gaze followed the swinging bag back [ ]
and his mouth hung open. "Where did yo[ ]
I already got the queen of spades from th[ ]
night, and I know the queen of diamonds a[ ]
of hearts from the other two murders are [ ]

"That's why it's a favor, Clive. It's [ ]
Can you just dust it for prints and let m[ ]
are any? If there are, I'll go through t[ ]
dence and submit it. I don't want to [ ]
right now over a simple playing ca[ ]
has no prints on it."

He held out his hand and she pl[ ]
which had surprisingly few line[ ]
Clive's hands looked soft, but h[ ]
fighter.

Crooking his finger, he said[ ]
it right now while you wait."

"Thank you so much. I ov[ ]

his stiff back into the lab and clicked the door shut behind them.

A lot of the forensics for LAPD was done at the county, but most of the larger divisions had their own fingerprint techs and other forensic specialists. The lab at the remodeled Northeast Division boasted a blood spatter and ballistics expert, so they didn't have to send out to county for that work.

Clive opened the bag and tipped the card onto a clean piece of paper, faceup. He dipped his brush into a container of black dust, like graphite, and shook off the excess. "You know, playing cards originally came from China, but the suits—the club, spade, diamond and heart—developed from Italian shapes, modified by the Germans and finally simplified by the French."

Kyra compressed her lips, flattening out her smile. Clive's brain contained a wealth of information, most of it trivial. She murmured, "That's fascinating."

"Don't pretend an interest you don't share, Kyra." He shook out the black particles from the brush onto the playing card. "My wife does the same thing, and I can spot disinterest a mile away. I'm used to it."

"I'm sorry. Distracted."

"That's all right." Clive lodged his tongue in the corner of his mouth for the delicate work before him. He'd been at this for as long as she'd been working with the department and probably a lot longer.

He used a pair of tweezers to lift the card and hold it under a light. "Nothing on this side, not even your prints."

"I lifted it off the ground with a pair of tongs from

the kitchen and slipped it into that plastic bag. I've been around the block a few times."

"Yes, you have." He flipped the card over so that the queen was no longer staring at her. "You're a therapist. What made you work with the police department?"

She watched as Clive repeated the process with the black powder on the flip side of the playing card. "I—I had a friend who was murdered in college. Her death affected us, affected me, so much I changed my major from pre-nursing to psychology. I did an internship with a therapist who worked with police officers, and my career just kind of took off from there."

"Very impressive." He eyed the card under a magnifying glass and sighed. "I'm afraid there are no prints on this card."

"Okay, that's fine. I'm sure this was just a coincidence. I mean there are lots of decks of cards floating around, aren't there?" She picked up the plastic bag and blew a puff of air into it to open it. "You can drop it back in here. I really appreciate your help, Clive. If there's anything I can do for you, let me know."

"I can't imagine anything, but I'll keep that in mind."

"Lunch, coffee." She drilled her finger into her chest. "I'm your girl."

He slid the card, blackened with fingerprint dust, back into the baggie. "I just ask that you don't spread it around that I'm available to do work under the radar… because I'm usually not."

"I won't." She traced her fingertip across the seam of her lips. "My lips are sealed."

They exited the lab together, and Clive pulled the door tight until he heard the lock click. He nodded in her direction. "See you later."

Clive took off down the hallway, his narrow shoulders set, his head tilted slightly to one side, the light above gleaming off his bald pate.

Clive's ready acquiescence to dust the card for prints surprised her, but he was nearing retirement and seemed a little less buttoned-up than usual.

She careened around the corner and nearly crashed into a solid mass of...man. "Oh, sorry."

Jake placed a hand on her waist to steady her and then dropped it as his eyebrows lowered. "Slow down. It's not like you're running out to a call or something."

Kyra folded her arms and stuffed the baggie into her purse. "Heard you got a trace on the phone."

"Heard you left with a reporter last night." He propped one broad shoulder against the wall, blocking her escape. Escape? Did she really want to escape Jake's presence? Not once she'd secured the queen of hearts in her purse.

"That's true. Megan Wright. She's my friend. I know you don't have any of those, but they're people you like and associate with and even do things for. You might try one sometime." She shook her finger at him. "I hear they even reduce stress."

The corner of his mouth twitched. "Believe it or not, I actually have a few of those."

"Coworkers and criminals don't count."

He let out a gurgle, which sounded suspiciously

like a laugh. "We got some good leads this morning. I wish... Where were you today?"

Had he been about to say he wished she'd been there? Progress. "Leads from the phone call?"

"Yeah, we have security videos to review in about an hour. The stores are sending them over." He glanced over his shoulder. "I think I owe you a lunch. I can fill you in."

"You mean the lunch you promised to drop on my desk in a brown paper bag at the office?"

"Did I mention a brown paper bag?" He pushed off the wall and jingled his car keys. "I mean a real lunch in a real restaurant, away from the station."

"Let's do it. You're going to have to get back here to watch that footage before you prep for the task force meeting. Four o'clock, right?" She took a step past him, and he swung in next to her.

"A lot of updates today but no ID on the victim from last night." He pushed open the door for her and held it as she walked through.

The man had his odd moments of chivalry. He even opened the door of his Crown Vic for her. He slammed it and circled around to the driver's side. As he got behind the wheel, he asked, "Any preferences?"

"Just no cop hangouts, even if they do give you the discount."

"The last place I want to go with you is a cop hangout." He cranked on the engine and the AC blasted her face.

She nudged the vent in his direction. "You don't want other cops to see you talking to me?"

"Would just prefer an opportunity to talk without getting interrupted every few minutes." He dialed down the air conditioning as he pulled out of the station's parking lot. "Looks like they've got that Malibu fire under control, although it did overtake the body dump site."

"So, the killer's fears were realized, after all. He must be resting easy now that he gets credit for his third victim." She clenched her jaw.

"First victim."

"What?" She jerked her head toward Jake. "What makes you think the woman last night was his first?"

"He made the rookie error of hiding her body too well so that she couldn't be found, or at least not found for several weeks or months. Also, the, um, decomposition of the body. I won't go into that before lunch."

"You don't have to. I get it." Her stomach still gurgled, and she didn't think it was from hunger.

Jake drove just a few blocks from the station and pulled into a strip mall. "There's a good Vietnamese pho place here, and if that doesn't interest you, there's pizza and a taco place."

"Pho sounds good. Not too hot for you on a warm day?"

"As long as the AC's on, I can handle it." He swung his car into a spot in front of a dry cleaner, and Kyra hopped out. When Jake opened the door of the restaurant, a rush of spicy smells made her mouth water.

"Hope you weren't expecting something fancy. You order at the counter and they'll bring your food to your table."

"That's most restaurants I go to." She flipped her ponytail over her shoulder and grabbed a laminated menu to study while they waited for the man in front of them asking a million questions.

After they both ordered, Jake placed their number on a table by the window while she filled up a paper cup with diet soda. Her blood fizzed as much as the soda. She couldn't wait to hear how the case was progressing, and she was getting a preview ahead of the rest of the task force—all for the price of some fish and chips last night, and Quinn vouching for her. All LAPD detectives revered the legendary Roger Quinn. Jake had proved to be no different, and her association with Quinn had given her status in Jake's eyes.

He returned with his own drink from the self-serve fountain machine and pulled out the plastic chair across from her. His large frame dwarfed the chair and the table.

He'd rolled up the sleeves of his light blue dress shirt, and the tail end of some ink crept onto his forearm. It looked like a snake or a tail and she wouldn't mind getting a look at the rest of it, but she averted her gaze to the tip of her straw and sucked down some soda.

"I heard the phone he called from wasn't a burner."

"You get right to the point." He folded his hands on the table; instead of being a prissy gesture as it would be for most men, it only emphasized his strength and masculinity as the veins popped over his corded forearms. "Info has a way of leaking, doesn't it?"

"But you never know if it's true or purely speculation and rumor."

"That particular piece of data is true." As the waitress approached the table to deliver their bowls of steaming pho, Jake moved their cups and silverware to make room.

The server placed the bowls in front of them and put down a silver tray containing little dishes of jalapeño, cilantro, bean sprouts and other ingredients to spice up the soup.

"After you." Jake nudged the tray toward her, and the little dishes trembled.

Using her fork, she added a few more ingredients to her pho, the steam from the bowl already making her sniff. "You haven't led me astray here, have you? I'm not going to take one spoonful of this pho and run screaming for the exit with steam coming from my ears, am I?"

He raised his eyebrows as he dropped a jalapeño into his soup. "For some reason, I thought you were a native Angeleno. Am I wrong? If not and you're like me, you were weaned on spicy food."

She did not want this conversation turning personal. She stirred her soup and slurped a sip from the large spoon. "Perfect."

"Glad you like it. You can always add more chili oil, if you like," he said, which he then proceeded to do.

"If the phone wasn't a burner, whose was it? If it belonged to the copycat, you'd have him in custody by now."

Jake patted his nose with his napkin. "It belongs to

Rachel Blackburn, a young community college student who works in a clothing and jewelry shop on Melrose. She lost the phone yesterday—or it was stolen from her."

"Hence the security cam footage for review. You're going to try to spot the moment someone picked up her phone."

"Exactly. She lost it somewhere on Melrose. She had it when she went into work, and didn't have it when she left work. She'd been to a few businesses along Melrose. We've pulled the video from those places."

"That's a huge lead."

"It gets better." Jake swirled his soda and took a sip, keeping her in suspense. "The shop also does piercings, and guess who got her nose pierced there a few weeks ago?"

Her own drink almost bubbled through her nose as she choked. "Kelsey?"

"That's right."

"One of the victims had her nose pierced at a shop on Melrose a few weeks before her murder, and the killer takes a phone from someone who works at the shop to call in another of his victims. He must live in, work in or frequent that area."

"Yeah, too bad it's so congested, but it's a start."

"It's a great start. You got lucky with that girl, Rachel Blackburn."

"She's a bright kid, interested in law enforcement. I told her to give me a call about a job with Dispatch. I know the sergeant and can put a word in for her."

Kyra dropped her spoon and stared at Jake, open-mouthed.

He jerked his head up and a bean sprout stuck to his chin. "What?"

"First of all—" Kyra tapped her own chin "—you have food on your face. Secondly, I didn't realize you were such a helpful person."

"Thanks." He swiped the bean sprout from his chin with a napkin. "I hate it when you have food on your face or in your teeth and nobody tells you. They just sit back and watch you make a fool of yourself."

She buried her chin in her palm. "That's nice of you to help out Rachel."

"Nice?" The color spiked in his cheeks, although that might be the jalapeño. "Nice had nothing to do with it. We need good people."

Jake didn't want to ruin his rep as a tough guy. She tilted her bowl to spoon up the rest of her pho. "Hopefully, that CCTV footage will reveal the phone thief... and the killer."

"I was thinking you might talk to Rachel. She's freaked out about being close to the copycat and the fact that he used her phone." He jabbed his spoon in her direction. "You do that sort of thing, too, right?"

"That sort of thing? Yes, I do. I'd be happy to talk to Rachel."

"All right then." He checked his cell phone, which had been on the table throughout lunch and buzzing periodically with text messages. "I'm going to get more soda for the road." He tapped his phone. "Just got a text from Billy that the video is queued up and ready for our viewing pleasure."

As she watched him walk to the soda machine, his gait sure and fluid like an athlete's, she felt a twist of disappointment in her belly. She would've liked to have learned a little more about Jake's personal life, his background. He was a Southern California boy, but where did he grow up? What had brought him to police work?

She wanted to learn those things about him, but he was too skilled a detective to allow the flow of information to go one way. And she had no intention of giving him the details of her background.

The secrecy made it hard to date, even harder to date someone in law enforcement. Of course, she was getting ahead of herself here. Nobody claimed, least of all Jake McAllister, that he was interested in dating her. She considered herself lucky he still didn't have daggers in his eyes when he looked at her.

He placed his cup on the edge of the table. "Do you want me to get you more soda before we leave?"

"Sure." She handed him her cup, and the tips of their fingers met on the damp surface.

Jake snatched the cup away and stalked toward the machine without even asking her what she was drinking.

She called after his back. "Diet, please."

He held up the cup and as he refilled her drink, she slipped her purse from the back of the chair and swung it to hitch over her shoulder.

As she did, it hit the chair, and some of the contents spilled out, including the plastic baggie with the card.

"Sorry." He began to crouch to collect her items.

"That's okay. I've got it." But she didn't have it. Jake had it.

He rose from his crouch, straightening to his full, intimidating height, the bag dangling from his fingertips, the flesh around his mouth white.

Through barely moving lips, he asked, "What the hell is this?"

Chapter Ten

Kyra's blue eyes met his, cool and unflinching chips of ice. "It's a card."

Anger whipped through his body, his veins sizzling with it. He exhaled a long breath through his mouth, which beat banging on the table with his fist. "Thanks, I know *what* it is. You know damned well I'm asking you where it came from and why it was fingerprinted."

"It's a long story, and you need to get back to the station." She tugged on the bag in his hand. "Do I still get a ride back?"

He should just leave her here. She had her phone. She could call up a car.

"I'll give you a ride." But if she thought she was going to retain possession of this card, she'd better think again.

He yanked the baggie from her fingers and stuffed it into his pocket. Then he grabbed his soda, with such a firm grip he almost popped off the lid, and pivoted on his heel.

He could hear the click of her heels following him

out of the restaurant as she called out cheerily to the staff behind the counter. "Thank you. Have a great day."

It was as if the hotter his rage burned, the colder she got in response. Did he expect tears? Did he want tears? The tears and recriminations from Tess had made him feel wanted. It was when his ex's feelings turned to disinterest—and another man—that he knew their marriage was over.

He stalked to the car, and habit compelled him to open the car door for her.

Halfway into the car, she cranked her head to the side. "I'll explain it to you. It's silly, simple."

He stuck his head in the car. "What makes you think I'm gonna believe anything you tell me?"

He slammed the door, shutting out her serene face with the slight curve to her full lips. He'd known women like her before. They sallied through life on their good looks, charming men into doing their bidding. Hell, she must've charmed Clive, of all people, into running a fingerprint test on that card.

He dropped onto the driver's seat and punched the ignition with his knuckle. He peeled out of the strip mall, the spicy food now burning a hole in his belly.

Kyra cleared her throat. "I found the card."

Jake tightened his jaw and clenched the steering wheel with both hands.

"I found it on the street, in the gutter, outside my apartment building." She shifted in her seat and smoothed her slacks against her thighs. "I didn't think it was a big deal or anything. Just one of those weird coincidences. If you look, it's not a brand-new card, not like the ones with the bodies."

The car jostled as he pulled into the parking lot of the station and Kyra bounced in her seat. He eased off the accelerator.

Turning to her, he threw the car into Park. "If it was no big deal, why hide it from me? I'm leading this task force. If I can't trust actual task force members, I'm in trouble."

She twisted her fingers in her lap, the first sign of agitation. "Look, I felt kind of silly. Why would the killer drop a playing card on my street in Santa Monica, of all places? I saw it and just reacted."

He flexed his fingers on the steering wheel. "And got Clive to run a test on it, on the sly."

She placed her hand on his arm. "Please don't blame Clive or get on his case for this. He's never done it before, and he made it clear he wouldn't do it again."

"What did he find?"

"Nothing." She lifted her shoulders. "There were no prints at all. Just my fevered imagination making connections in my overactive brain."

He brushed his hand against the outside of his pocket, where the plastic crinkled. "Kind of a strange coincidence."

"Just what I thought."

He pulled out the baggie. "Do you want it back?"

"That's okay." She lifted one shoulder. "Keep it, throw it away, whatever."

"All right, then. Um, I'm sorry I may have overreacted back there." He exited the vehicle and waited for Kyra to come around to his side.

"No problem. I get it." She pressed her hand against his back, giving him a little shove. "You have some footage to review."

"If you're not busy, do you want to join us?" He dug his teeth into his bottom lip. He was just trying to make amends for his previous outburst. Maybe she'd see that and decline.

"I would like to join you, thanks."

Did he really think she wouldn't jump at the chance to insert herself further into this investigation? Did he mind? After all, surveying video could be mind-numbing work and the more people on deck, the better.

As they returned to the station, their appearance raised a few eyebrows. Jake put a scowl on his face to ward off any ribbing from his coworkers later. He called out a few names as he marched through the station and held up his finger. "Follow me to the war room."

Brandon and his team had already set up several computers and loaded the footage on them. Before he'd left for lunch, Jake had instructed Brandon to divvy up the video between the different computers so that individual teams would all be reviewing a variety of times and locations.

Standing in the middle of the room, he directed traffic, assigning teams of two to each computer. As they huddled over the monitors, someone tapped him on the shoulder.

He didn't have to turn around to know who it was.

The sweet, dusky smell of roses hung around Kyra as if she crushed them against her skin every day.

Twisting his head over his shoulder, he said, "You can hang out with me until Billy gets here."

He took a seat in front of his computer, security footage from Melrose Avenue queued up to start. He taped a picture of Rachel on the monitor next to his. "This is Rachel—black, shoulder-length hair, sleeve of tattoos on her right arm, piercings, about your height, medium frame."

Kyra pulled a chair next to his and settled into it, propping her elbow on the table and balancing her chin on her palm. Her ponytail slipped over her shoulder, the ends of it tickling the keyboard. "What are we looking at now?"

"This is Rachel's afternoon coffee run. By this time, she's already had morning coffee at the same shop, been to work, gone out to lunch and visited her friend in another store. This is her last stop before going back to work." His hand hovered over the mouse. "Ready?"

"Ready." Her nostrils flared slightly and she parted her lips.

Jake clicked the start arrow on the footage, which Brandon's team had queued up about ten minutes before the time Rachel had given them. They watched the busy shop as people ordered their coffee and food at the counter and drifted away to wait for their orders.

The cameras pointed at the registers only, so any other customer interaction they hoped to see would have to be in the background, beyond the people ordering. Another team was studying the footage from outside the store.

They sat still, side by side, Kyra barely breathing. Her proximity overwhelmed his senses, and then her knee touched his pant leg.

Jake rubbed his eyes and brought his face closer to the monitor. About seven minutes in, Kyra jabbed him with her elbow. "Is that Rachel? I see black hair."

"That's Rachel." Jake stalled the video and took screen shots of Rachel's progress through the store. "Too bad she didn't use her phone to buy the coffee."

"She told you that already?"

"Yeah, like I said—" he tapped the side of his head "—she's a sharp girl."

Kyra squinted at the screen. "I'm trying to figure out if I can see her phone in her purse but no luck. I have a pocket on the outside of my bag where I keep my cell. You can see the outline of the phone when you look at my purse."

"Is that on the other side of where you keep your gun?" He raised one eyebrow.

"You're not supposed to be able to see the outline of that."

"I'm a cop. I can spot a purse with a gun pouch a mile away."

She poked him in the leg. "Our girl is up."

Rachel stepped to the counter and ordered from the female barista, exchanging a few words. She swiped her debit card to pay for the purchase, then wandered out of the camera's view, stepping back and to the left to wait for her coffee.

The camera didn't have a clear view of the pickup area. Baristas shoved drinks and little bags of food onto the counter, where impatient, caffeine-deprived hands grabbed them. Jake jabbed a finger at the monitor. "That's Rachel. Notice the tat on her wrist? The nails?"

"We can't see her purse, can't see anyone around her." Kyra slumped in her chair. "I guess I expected to discover someone clearly reaching a hand in her bag and snatching her phone. We can't even tell if she had her cell phone going into Uncommon Grounds."

"We can't—" he swept one arm to the side "—but maybe someone else will pick up something."

As Jake clicked on the timer to run the tape back to see if they'd overlooked something, Billy swept into the war room. He raised one eyebrow when he homed in on Jake's partner and then shrugged.

Clapping his hands, Billy shouted, "How close are you to being done, and has anyone found anything?"

His words were met with a few grumbles and groans and not one eureka.

One cop in the corner raised his hand. "We had Rachel's morning coffee run, and we saw her on the phone. So, she had it then."

"All right. All right." Billy stepped up to a clean whiteboard and made a notation. "Time stamp?"

The officer gave him a time, and Billy ran down the whiteboard with a red marker as others called out their times and findings. With Rachel still in possession of her phone at lunch, Billy circled around to Jake.

and Kyra. "Which brings us to you two for the coffee break after lunch."

Jake leaned back in his chair, crossing his arms behind his head. "We didn't see anything—no evidence of her phone, no unusual encounters."

"Anyone have footage from the sidewalk of Rachel's return to work? I think that's our last piece since she said she didn't have the phone when she was getting ready to leave for work for the day." Billy swiveled his head from side to side, and the room remained silent.

Jake pushed out of his chair. "Brandon, who had that last part of Rachel's timeline?"

Brandon popped up, red faced, from where he'd been crawling on the floor connecting cables. "We don't have it. It's the same camera from the street where we watched her go in for lunch and then into the coffeehouse, but for some reason there's no footage from later that day."

Jake ran a hand through his hair, the ends of his fingers tingling with frustration. Unlike Kyra, he hadn't expected to see the culprit lifting Rachel's phone, but accurate footage showing a clear timeline would be good.

"I have a question." Kyra wiggled her fingers in the air. "For those of you who saw Rachel with her phone, was she on it or did you see it in her bag or pocket?"

Billy asked around the room, and the teams that had seen her with the phone reported that she had the phone in her hand.

Picking up on Kyra's train of thought, Jake asked,

"When Rachel got off the phone, did she put it in her purse? Zip it up so nobody could get to it?"

One of the female officers spoke up. "We saw her texting for several minutes while she was eating lunch outside with her friend. When she was done, she put the phone next to her on the bench. I'd never do that. When I saw her, I thought to myself that was a good way to lose your phone. When she left, she did drop it into her purse, no side pocket or anything like that."

"So, you think she might have left it out at a later time and somebody picked it up." Jake rubbed his chin. "Nobody had to pick her pocket or lift it from her purse if she just left it sitting somewhere."

Billy put a big red arrow pointing at Rachel's lunch and another aimed at her store at three o'clock. "She lost the phone between here and here."

Kyra nudged Jake. "That's us. Can we play it back again?"

"Sure." Jake raised his voice. "Thanks for your hard work, everyone. We'll coordinate with the West Hollywood Sheriff's Station, and do some more canvassing in that area. It has another connection to one of our victims, so it's a hot spot for us. Leave any stills you took with Cool Breeze, and you can take off."

Chairs scraped and empty soda cans hit the recycling bins, and the officers shuffled out of the room.

Billy scribbled a few more words on his whiteboard timeline and pointed the marker at Jake. "Mind if I lean over your shoulders?"

"C'mon over." Jake scooted his chair closer to

Kyra's. "I'm glad Kyra was here to help out. I didn't realize you were going to be so late."

"Had some leads on the identity of our Malibu fire victim." Billy clicked his tongue as he pulled up a chair and squeezed next to Jake. "Nothing panned out. That poor woman still doesn't have a name."

"You checked out the missing persons report that looked promising?"

"Chased it down. Showed the sister a picture of our victim, and she failed to make the ID."

"He doesn't seem to be targeting runaways, does he?" Kyra drummed her fingers close to Jake's hand. "Marissa and Kelsey weren't runaways."

Billy lifted one shoulder. "Maybe he's not targeting anyone. He sees an opportunity and takes it. That's why the West Hollywood area is so important. Kelsey got a piercing at Rachel's shop, and Rachel's phone was stolen by the killer, or at least someone connected to the killer."

"I think that was definitely our guy on the phone last night." Jake clicked the mouse. "You ready to put eyeballs on this?"

He'd queued up the video to start seconds before Rachel entered Uncommon Grounds. When the action rolled, Jake poked his finger at the screen. "You can see her arm behind this guy in line."

Three sets of eyes studied Rachel's progress through the line and her turn at the counter.

"Wait," Kyra shouted, and both Jake and Billy jumped. "She has her purse open to get her wallet. That looks like the edge of a phone right there."

As Jake leaned in, he felt Kyra's warm breath on his cheek. "You're right. That's her phone. Good job."

Rachel shoved her card in the chip reader and pulled it out. She tucked the card back into her purse without touching her phone. She stepped out of the camera's view to wait for her drink.

Kyra sighed. "Anything could be happening off camera."

Rachel reached in to grab her drink, and they couldn't even see her purse or her other hand.

Kyra circled an area on the screen that showed Rachel's other arm behind her body. "She could be holding a phone there."

"We can ask her." Jake backed up and snapped a picture of Rachel's open purse with a gleaming corner of her phone visible. "I told you, she's a bright girl. She might remember what happened in the coffee place the moment before or after she picked up her drink—someone bumping into her, some distraction. I'll give her a call when I can."

Billy stood up and stretched. "You canceled the task force meeting today?"

"I figured everyone got a good update in here. I'm going to get on the phone with the Sheriff's Department and let them know we'll be nosing around Melrose."

"And I have a few clients to see later." Kyra shoved back from the desk, linked her fingers and stretched her arms in front of her. "Thanks for allowing me to view the footage."

"You provided some good insight. I don't think I

could've made out anything in a woman's purse." Jake felt Billy jab two fingers between his shoulders, and he shrugged him off.

Kyra pushed to her feet and patted her purse. "I left the case for my sunglasses in your car."

"I'll take you down to get them." Jake flicked a finger at the printouts in Billy's hand. "You have everything you need?"

"I sure do."

Jake walked Kyra from the room, and they went down to the parking lot. He unlocked the car, and she ducked inside to retrieve her case.

She held it up over the roof of the car. "Got it."

"Where's your car?"

"I parked it on the street. The lot was crowded, and I didn't want to take up a space."

"I'll walk you out there." He ignored the look she shot him. He knew it was still daylight and they were in front of a police station, but old habits died hard.

"Not necessary, but okay." She retrieved her car keys and jingled them. "No keyless ignition for me yet. My car's ancient."

When they got to the curb where she'd parked her car, Kyra slid forward and slammed her hands against the passenger window.

"Are you all right?" Jake grabbed her arm. Her skin felt clammy beneath his touch.

"I—I'm fine." She twisted away from him and pushed off the car, where her hands had left moist prints on the glass. "I'm so clumsy, I slipped on the curb."

The last thing he'd call Kyra Chase was clumsy. Jake glanced down at the perfectly dry curb without a crack in place. Behind his own sunglasses, he watched her smiling lips tremble.

"You don't seem fine. Did you almost faint or something? Do you want me to get you water?"

"For a little slip?" She clicked the remote on her key fob. "I'm good. Thanks again for including me today."

She stood with her back against the passenger door, her shoulders squared, a bright, fake smile plastered to her face.

"I'll make sure you get to the other side okay." He cupped her elbow and walked her around to the driver's side.

She slid into her car and slammed the door on him. When she started her engine, she buzzed down the window. "Thanks, again."

Jake nodded and hesitated, but Kyra pulled out her phone and bent her head over it, her fingers tapping furiously.

He forced himself to walk away from her car. He couldn't stand there all day looking at her through the window. Raising his hand, he stalked back to the station parking lot. Before he walked into the building, he twisted his head to the side to find Kyra's car still idling at the curb. The white oval through the window looked like her face.

She was still watching him?

When he walked into the station, Jake bolted up three flights of stairs and charged into the lunchroom, which had a view of the street.

As he squinted through the tinted glass, Kyra got out of her car, went around to the passenger side, crouched down and reached beneath the car's chassis.

Jake gritted his teeth. What the hell was she lying about this time?

Chapter Eleven

Kyra clutched the queen of diamonds in her hand and smeared her thumb across the glossy surface to sweep off the particles of dirt clinging to it. Fingerprints didn't concern her this time. He'd left none on the other card, and she couldn't run to Clive with another playing card, anyway.

Could she run to Jake?

She glanced at the white expanse of the station. Would CCTV help to identify who'd dropped the playing card next to her car? If she'd parked in the station's lot, there would've been footage for sure. That would be less likely out here in the street.

She dropped the card onto her console and gripped the steering wheel, resting her forehead on her bunched knuckles. How did the killer know who she was, where she lived, what car she drove? It didn't make sense.

Finding this second card screamed loud and clear that the first card had not been a coincidence. What had Quinn always told her? There are no coincidences in law enforcement.

She had to tell Jake. These cards could lead to the

capture of the copycat killer. The task force had precious little to go on right now.

If she told him, she could still keep her other secret. She could claim she had no idea why someone, possibly this killer, was leaving playing cards for her.

She'd tell Jake…for the sake of the case, for the sake of those victims. She noted the time on the car's clock and shifted into Drive. First she'd see her clients and touch base with Quinn. She hadn't even told him about the first card.

She headed back toward the coast where a gray line of haze sat on the horizon. The Malibu Canyon fire still burned, but the firefighters had contained it, which meant no more nonstop news coverage—until the next wildfire blazed forth. The Santa Ana winds worried the tops of the palm trees and sucked the moisture out of the air, but no new fires had popped up.

When would that body from last night have been discovered had the fire not whipped through the canyon? The copycat may have been more content to wait if it hadn't. He wouldn't have put himself at risk with that phone call.

The copycat had exposed himself in a way The Player never would've done. That meant law enforcement could count on more mistakes from him. Like leaving two playing cards for her? A number of other people could be responsible for that, including a few of the miscreants she'd stumbled across in the foster care system.

By the time she reached her office in Santa Monica, the sun had started dipping into the ocean, its rays filtering through the smoke from the fire to create an orange streak across the sky.

She cruised down Wilshire and pulled into the parking lot of a two-story office building that she and another therapist shared with a realty office, an aesthetician, a pizza place and a hairstylist.

She and her office roomie, as she called Candace, shared the space, which consisted of a waiting room where they could conduct groups and an inner office for private sessions. They scheduled their clients at different times and used the same space. Saved a lot of money, especially in this area, and Kyra spent a lot of her time at various police stations.

She jogged up the stairs and used her key to unlock the office. She left the door unlocked and retreated to what she and Candace called the treatment room.

A small desk neither of them used huddled in the corner while comfortable chairs with colorful cushions took up the space in the middle of the room.

She knew which chair her next client would take. He always sat in the same one—they all did.

The door clicked in the outer office, and Kyra smoothed back her hair and relaxed the muscles of her face. After the day she'd had, she needed therapy probably more than her clients did. Not that she hadn't already had plenty of it.

The red light above the door flashed, and Kyra answered the call—a cop who, like so many before him, had let the job and alcohol destroy his marriage.

An hour later, Kyra folded her hands in her lap. "We're out of time, Evan."

He sat back in his chair and ran a hand over his close-cropped hair. "That went by fast. It always does."

"I'll see you next time." Kyra rose to her feet and opened the door to the outer office. She accepted all payments online now, which cut out the awkwardness of taking a check or cash after a session.

Evan stopped at the door, close enough for her to smell the faded mint from the chewing gum he used as a substitute for alcohol. "I heard about a third body in this copycat case. I also heard you're on the task force."

She nodded once, hoping to end the conversation before it started.

"How do you like working with J-Mac?" Evan's stocky frame filled the door.

"Excuse me?" Her fingers twisted the handle. She never talked about her personal life with clients. After six months of treatment, Evan should know that rule by now, especially as he'd tried to get too friendly before and she'd put him in his place.

He seemed to flinch at her cold tone. Good.

"Just wondering what the guy was like. Heard he was a great detective but not easy to work with." Evan lifted a square shoulder.

"Yeah, I really wouldn't know. I work with the victims."

"Next time then." Evan thrust out his hand and she shook it.

"Next time." Many clients went in for the hug at the end of a session, but not usually cops. Kyra generally let the clients dictate the level of closeness they needed at the end of an appointment, and guys like

Evan preferred the firm handshake to show that they were back in control, even after an emotional hour that sometimes included tears.

When the door to the outside closed, Kyra returned to the office to turn off the lights. During her session with Evan, her next client had canceled, which gave Kyra a chance to get to Quinn's place earlier.

She perched on the edge of the desk and called him.

"What's wrong?"

"There's nothing wrong." The lie sounded thin. "Just a few things I want to run past you. Do you want me to pick up dinner?"

"No need. Rose across the channel dropped off a lasagna. I can't eat the whole thing myself."

"Perfect." She smiled into the phone. "Rose, huh? Didn't she just lose her husband the movie producer last year?"

"She did, but don't get any ideas." He coughed. "And you'd better be prepared to tell me what's wrong when you get here. You're an expert at keeping secrets, but not from me."

"I have no intention of keeping any secrets from you, and I also don't need to worry you over the phone."

She heard a sharp intake of breath. "Do I need to worry?"

"See what I mean?" She hopped off the desk. "Heat up that lasagna. You got stuff for salad?"

"Yes, hurry up."

Kyra ended the call and sucked in her bottom lip. She didn't want Quinn to be concerned about her, but she wanted to bounce this off him before she went to Jake—and she had to go to Jake.

She locked up the office and made the short drive from Santa Monica to Venice—short in distance. The traffic made the journey crawl.

By the time she knocked on Quinn's door, the sun had set and her stomach was grumbling. She reached for the door handle in case Quinn wasn't up to the trek across his living room floor.

He flung it open before she could tell if it was locked or not. He'd slicked back his gray hair and even trimmed his wild eyebrows.

She kissed his worn cheek. "You look nice. Did you make an effort for Rose?"

"Stop." He waved his hand. "Tell me what's going on before you scurry off to the kitchen. The food can wait."

She sniffed the garlic-scented air. "Apparently not."

She followed him to his chair and sat across from him on the love seat. She pulled the queen of diamonds from her purse. "Found this by my car this afternoon, on the ground."

"And put your prints all over it." He snapped his fingers, and she placed the card on his outstretched palm.

"There won't be any prints."

"And how do you know that? People make mistakes." He turned the card over.

"Because that's not the first one I found, and the queen of hearts didn't have prints." She held her breath and watched the lines on his craggy face deepen, a needle of guilt pricking the back of her neck.

"Where and when did you find the other card?"

"On the ground, near the dumpster behind my apartment building—queen of hearts that time." She raised her finger. "I did scoop that one up and had the fingerprint tech at the Northeast Division test it. You remember Clive? He's still there."

"So, you turned it in to McAllister and the task force." He sank back in his chair, tapping the edge of the card on his knee.

"Not exactly."

"Keeping secrets again, Kyra? You don't belong on the task force if you're keeping secrets. That could put someone's life in danger. They need every clue right now, and this is a clue. They both are."

"I know that now after finding the second card." She spread her hands. "I thought the one at my apartment was a coincidence."

"You know what I told you about coincidences in investigations."

She repeated with him. "There are no coincidences in law enforcement."

She brushed a hand across her slacks. "I didn't want to raise any alarms with that first card. Clive didn't find any prints on it and there are no cameras at my place, so I figured it didn't matter."

A spark lit Quinn's faded blue eyes as his gaze drilled into her.

She rose from the love seat and circled around it. "Then when I found the second card, I knew it had meaning. But what? This copycat killer can't know who I am."

"Who says the copycat killer left the cards?"

She linked her hands in front of her and twisted her fingers. "You mean it could be someone else taking advantage of the situation to torture me?"

"Anyone come to mind?" He snapped the card on the coffee table.

Kyra folded her arms and dug her fingers into her biceps. "You're not talking about Matt, are you?"

"Just throwing it out there. He saw the news and thought he'd poke at you. You know he's capable."

"I know Matt is capable of just about anything, but he'd also like nothing more than for me to reach out to him to find out if he's playing tricks." She whipped her head back and forth. "I'm not going to do that."

"And you shouldn't." Quinn prodded the card with his finger. "Where's the other one? You said there were two cards."

"Jake has the other one." She shoved one hand in the pocket of her slacks in a nonchalant pose.

"I thought you said he didn't know about the cards."

"The queen of hearts fell out of my purse when we were at lunch, so I had to tell him about it."

Quinn grimaced with one side of his mouth. "That must've gone over well."

"He wasn't happy, if that's what you mean." Kyra marched into the kitchen. "I don't know about you, but I'm starving and that lasagna smells good."

"He accused you of keeping it from him, being deceptive."

Kyra bent forward and peered at the lasagna heating up on the middle rack, the heat from the oven warming her face. "Of course, he did, but I explained that I brought it in for prints and that I believed it was just a coincidence. I did believe that."

"You don't toy with a man like McAllister. I'm sure you heard about his run-in with that therapist. You must've heard about it. You were working with her."

"Not on that, I wasn't. I never would've tried to get a lighter sentence for that guy. Jake was right to be angry. I was there when it happened." She banged through Quinn's cupboard to retrieve a colander, a large bowl, a knife and a cutting board.

By the time she'd chopped the salad veggies, the oven timer had dinged, signaling the lasagna was heated through. Kyra pulled the dish out of the oven, and Quinn joined her and grabbed a couple of plates from the cupboard.

He said, "I'll set the table."

A few minutes later, they sat across from each other, and Kyra smiled, her eyes misty. "Just like old times."

"The only thing missing is Charlotte." Quinn rested a hand on the empty place mat beside him.

"Charlotte and my bad attitude." Kyra stabbed her fork into her salad.

"Oh, you still have plenty of attitude." Quinn shook his own fork at her. "When are you going to tell Jake about the second card and why you hid it from him?"

"Soon." She studied a dripping tomato skewered on the end of her fork. "And I'll think of something to tell him—anything but the truth."

"You think you'll get away with that with him?"

Quinn's thin lips twisted. "You won't have to tell him the truth because he'll figure it out one of these days… all on his own."

JAKE HUNCHED OVER his computer, his third Diet Coke of the afternoon pumping caffeine through his system. A search of Kyra Chase didn't get him very far. She'd graduated from UCLA with a degree in psychology, and then went to Cal State LA part-time to get her master's in clinical psychology while she worked full-time. Her work ethic and ambition didn't surprise him. Something was driving her, but her background didn't give any hints what that was.

She avoided social media, which was probably a good idea given her line of work. He avoided it, too. He needed suspects tracking him down about as much as Kyra needed clients tracking her down.

He did see where Charlotte Quinn had dedicated one of her books to K.C., her favorite therapist. The connection between Kyra and the Quinns was real, but why had she lied about working with him on a case? And why did Quinn back her up?

Kyra could've lied about that for his benefit, trying to make herself more professionally acceptable in his eyes.

Jake growled to the empty war room. "Nah. That woman doesn't care what you think of her."

He sat back in his chair, rubbed his burning eyes and tossed back the rest of his drink. Propping his feet onto his desk, he dragged one of The Player files into his lap.

People had started calling this killer The Copycat

or The Copycat Player. Despite a few unique touches, he did have The Player's MO down.

Why that killer? Why now? There were many cold cases in LA. Why did he choose that one? Jake refused to believe The Player had come out of retirement, even though he could still be young enough to hunt.

He opened the thick file in his lap and scanned the familiar contents. As scant as it was, most of this stuff—the autopsies and the evidence—was online. Roger Quinn appeared older than his age. Caring for his wife before she died must've taken its toll, but Jake could guarantee The Player took a whole other kind of toll on the old detective.

He flipped toward the back of the file, perusing notes about the victims and their families. He smoothed his hand over a crumpled page with a black, angry scrawl at the bottom. Squinting, he made out the word *Denied.*

His gaze tracked to the top of the page. One of The Player's victims, Jennifer Lake, had left a young daughter behind, no father on the scene. Roger Quinn had gotten involved and had been advocating for this girl to the point where he and his wife wanted to adopt her instead of sending her into LA's foster care system. Ultimately, their request had been rejected.

With his heart pounding in his chest, Jake scrambled through the additional pages in the file, searching for information on Jennifer Lake's daughter. He dropped the file on the floor and dug into the stack on the corner of his desk.

He flipped open the one on Jennifer and stared at

the picture of the pretty blonde. It was one of those cheesy modeling photos for an acting portfolio—ruby-red lips, heavily made-up eyes, styled hair. Jennifer had been an aspiring actress and part-time call girl. It had been the latter profession that had gotten her into trouble. She'd been twenty-five years old at the time of her murder, with an eight-year old daughter in tow. That daughter—he skimmed down the page with his finger—was named Marilyn Monroe Lake.

He slumped in his chair. Who the hell named their kid Marilyn Monroe? At least she'd given the kid a nickname.

He thumbed through a few more pages and froze as another photo spilled out of the pile—this one a natural pose of a fresh-faced young woman, her blond hair in a ponytail, her wide aquamarine blue eyes startling in her pale face.

Jake grabbed his bag and slung it over his shoulder. He waved to the guys on the night shift and climbed into his car. The adrenaline in his body weighted his foot on the gas pedal and he sped down the freeway to the coast in record time. He buzzed down his window to gulp in the sea-scented air that caressed his hot face.

Apartments lined the streets in this area of Santa Monica, about two miles up from the beach. Crime came at you here from the transients and the tweakers looking for some quick cash. Jake hugged the side of the street, looking for a gap in the row of cars parked for the night.

He squeezed into a spot and exited his vehicle. The older apartment complexes on this street didn't boast any security except for the lock on your front door. He breezed into the small courtyard, two stories of apartments on either side of him for a total of eight places.

A quick glance at the apartment numbers on the side of the building told him her place occupied the worst possible spot for safety—in the back, near the carport. As he strode toward the rear of the complex, he cocked his head at the sound of jingling keys. As he rounded the corner to her front door, his leg brushed the spiky fronds of a sago palm. After he moved past it, the frond snapped back into place.

The slight noise was enough. Kyra jerked her head to the side, her hand reaching for her gun pouch, her eyes widening at the sight of him, registering recognition and then suspicion.

Jake stopped several feet from her, planting his wing tips on the cement walkway. "Hello, Mimi."

Chapter Twelve

Kyra dropped her key chain. Despite her weak knees, she did a quick dip to retrieve it. Her brain whirred for several seconds as she gathered herself. She knew it was pointless to deny it, but years of self-preservation kicked in.

She faced him, one side of her mouth quirking into a smile. "You've got the wrong person. I'm Kyra, not Mimi."

"You're Kyra Chase now…" He squared his shoulders as if ready to do battle. "Twenty years ago, you were Marilyn Monroe Lake, a frightened eight-year-old girl who'd just lost her mother to a killer."

"So sad for Marilyn Monroe Lake." Turning her back on him, she shoved her key into the dead bolt and clicked it. What else had he discovered about her? Quinn had been right about J-Mac. She shouldn't have tried to play him.

As she thrust open the door, she felt Jake's presence over her shoulder. And now she couldn't get rid of him.

"Are you going to invite me in to discuss this? Discuss why you lied to me?" He placed his hand flat against the door, holding it wide.

"Do I have a choice?" She floated inside her apartment, dropped the keys into a basket on the low wall that separated her small dining area from the entrance hall and placed her purse next to the basket. "You can close and dead bolt the door behind you."

The door was shut, and the gentleness of it caused her more dread than if he'd slammed it. Would he kick her off the task force? She couldn't allow that to happen. She'd use every favor, every tool in her arsenal, to keep her place on the task force.

She spun around, her fists clenching at her sides. "Why are you snooping into my background? Do you do that for every task force member or just the ones you don't want to work with?"

He clasped a hand on the back of his neck, and for the first time she noticed the weariness in his handsome face, the lines on the sides of his mouth etched deep, the hazel eyes, dark and unfathomable. "Is that what you think? Have I really shown you that I don't want you on the task force? Don't want to work with you? I invited you to survey the video footage with me today. I drove you to the murder scene last night."

She blinked her eyes. And she might've just messed up. She should've listened to Quinn. When had he ever steered her wrong?

"Besides," he sighed, and sank onto her couch, grabbing a throw pillow and dragging it into his lap, "I didn't discover you were Marilyn Lake by looking in your background, although I tried. Your name and ID change are pretty thorough. There is nothing online that links you to that little girl."

"I hired the best to clean my background." She perched on the arm of the chair across from him. "Then how'd you find out and why were you digging into my past?"

"You raised my suspicions. You couldn't have worked with Quinn on any of his cases. He retired before you would've been old enough to work."

"Oh, yeah." She chewed on her bottom lip. She should've had a better story prepared, but she didn't know Jake was going to drop in on Quinn the same night she was bringing him dinner. "That was it? I told you I knew Charlotte, had been her resource for one of her books."

"That wasn't all." He tossed aside the handmade pillow she'd gotten in Guatemala with no apparent regard for the effort required to bring that pillow home. "Today, when I walked you to your car and you stumbled, I watched you from the station as you got out of your car and retrieved something from the gutter."

Kyra felt the blood drain from her face, and she pressed her fingers against her cool cheek. There really was no fooling this man. Of course, she'd planned to tell him about the second card, but she'd had no intention of telling him she'd found it beside her car and had hidden it from him.

"That's what convinced you to look into my past?"

He nodded, his face tight and wary.

For the first time in a long time she felt the burn of regret for her deception, and it wasn't just because she'd been found out. She had the feeling that Jake had endured lies from others, and now she'd become like everyone else in his life.

She didn't want to be like everyone else for him.

Sliding down the arm of the chair to settle onto the cushion, she asked, "You said you didn't find out who I was by looking into my background."

"That's right." He braced one foot against the edge of the coffee table. "I discovered your identity by looking at The Player case file."

Tilting her head, she wrapped her ponytail around her hand. "There are no pictures of me as a child in that file and no indication that I changed my name. Quinn assured me of that."

"That's true, but there is a story about a hardened detective and his wife who were so overcome with pity for a motherless girl that they sought to adopt her and keep her out of the system." He shrugged his broad shoulders.

"You made the connection between that poor, pitiable little girl and me?" She shook her head. "That's some hunch, Detective."

"It was a hunch that didn't bear out when I discovered Jennifer's daughter's name was Marilyn Lake, but then I saw this." He pulled a folded sheet of paper from his pants pocket and shook it out. "Unmistakably you."

Kyra hunched forward and snatched the paper from his hand. Her mother's eyes, so full of hope and optimism, met hers, and the scent of her mother's floral perfume overwhelmed her. Her chest tightened, and her throat closed. The paper floated from her hand as she gasped for breath.

She felt herself tumbling, tumbling through time and fear and sadness. The aching sadness gripped her belly and clawed at the carefully constructed facade that she'd been building for the past ten years since she graduated from high school and changed her name. The wound gaped open and the contents of her pathetic, tortured life began to seep out.

She clutched her midsection and moaned, toppling onto her side. As she began to slide off the couch, into the narrow space between the couch and the coffee table, strong hands pinched her shoulders.

She heard her name from far away... *Mimi, Mimi, it's me and you, Mimi. You're my little good-luck charm.*

"Kyra, Kyra. Are you all right?"

Rough, blunt fingers, not her mother's cool, delicate ones with the coral polish on the tips, brushed her cheek. The male voice, low and urgent, pierced the fog of her consciousness.

"Kyra, lie back. I'm going to get you some water, or something stronger if I can find it."

He left her, and the haze began to clear from her brain. As Jake knocked around her kitchen, she grabbed the arm of the chair and pulled herself to an upright position.

She smoothed her hand over her hair and dashed the moisture from her cheeks.

By the time Jake made it back to the living room with a glass of water in one hand and a measure of something that looked like apple cider vinegar in the other, her breathing had returned to normal, although her heart still galloped in her chest.

He held up the glass in his right hand. "Water or some really old Scotch?"

"I'll take the water. I'm fine." When she took the glass from his hand, their fingers brushed and she wanted to drop the glass and grab on to his warm, strong hand for dear life.

She gulped back the water. "I'm really okay. It's just that I hadn't seen that photo in a long time. It brought back…memories."

He crouched at her feet and rested a hand on her bouncing knee. "Terrifying, tragic ones. I'm sorry I sprang it on you like that. It's a beautiful picture of your mother. The second I laid eyes on it I knew you were her daughter. You look so much alike, except for the eyes."

Her gaze darted to the picture on the floor. "The eyes? Really? People always used to tell us we had the exact same color of eyes. She assured me that it would be her eyes that would propel her to stardom, just like Liz Taylor's. My mother lived for old Hollywood."

"The color and the shape are almost identical. It's the expression that's different." He pinched the corner of the paper between two fingers. "Hers lack your cynicism, your distrust, your worldliness."

"Maybe if my mother had possessed a little more cynicism and a little less trust, she'd be alive today." Kyra's nose stung and she swiped the back of her hand beneath it. "You must've read about her extracurricu-

activities. She took the idea of the casting couch a
[t]oo far."

that." Jake squeezed her knee and backed
in a crouch. "Was your mother from
was a young mother. What about

between her knees and lifted
seventeen when she had
father was. Her small
off for Hollywood

ne
back
cret."

ason why
at task force
families." She
of it landing in

t on this task force,
ngs to get assigned,
ows how I feel about

of the first two killings,
. I knew we had a copycat
wanted to be on the inside."
d thrust out her chin. "You

Under the same circumstances,
to drag me away from the inves-
ed the sexy stubble on his chin. "I
ut why you didn't tell me your con-
se. Why hide it?"
a V with two fingers and pointed them
s why."

"Except Quinn." He dragged a hand through his messy, dark locks. "You didn't think it was important information given the nature of this case?"

"Important to me."

"Important to the task force lead? In fact—" stuffed her Guatemalan pillow behind his lower b

"—I would've thought you'd be eager to tell me

"Eager? Whatever for? It's my deep, dark s One of her deep, dark secrets.

"It would've given you cred, another re you belonged on the task force."

"The only reason I need for being on th is my experience with victims and their took another quick gulp of water, half her lap.

"You can't tell me you didn't wan Kyra. I know you pulled some str especially because Castillo kn working with therapists."

"When I heard the details it hit me like a ton of bricks on our hands and, yeah, I She hardened her jaw a can understand that."

"I do understand it you wouldn't be able tigation." He scratc just can't figure o nection to the ca She formed at him. "That

arou

He blinked. "What?"

"That look in your eyes—pity, sorrow. The only reason discomfort isn't in the mix is because you're a cop and accustomed to dealing with victims." She drew back her shoulders. "I'm not a victim."

Jake threw up his hands. "Nobody said you were— not in the sense that you can't take care of yourself or that you feel put-upon, but The Player put you in a particular class. You're the daughter of a murder victim. That's not your shame to bear."

"Shame?" She jumped up from the chair and did a quick, agitated trip around the small living room. "I'm not ashamed of my mother or the fact that she was murdered, but I don't want that to inform my entire life."

"And yet here you are."

"Excuse me?"

"Here you are—a therapist, specializing in victims' rights, cops, working on task forces. You're going to tell me your past didn't inform those choices?"

"It did. Of course it did." She jabbed a finger into her chest. "I'm good at what I do. I'm good at what I do because I can empathize like nobody's business. When I tell the daughter of a murder victim that I know how she feels, I ain't lying. When I express sympathy for the loss of someone's daughter, like the Lindquists yesterday, they can hear the truth in my voice, feel it in my touch."

"I agree with everything you say. I've seen you in action." He'd twisted in his seat to follow her progress across the room. One arm lay across the back of the couch, his sleeve rolled up to reveal the tail end of that tattoo. "I'm a cop because my old man was a cop. I have anger management issues because my old man had anger management issues. I have a… We're products of our upbringing and our backgrounds, and having a mother who was the victim of one of the most notorious serial killers in LA is a helluva legacy to carry around."

"Okay, what do you want me to do?" She tapped her chest twice with the palms of her hands and then spread her arms wide. "Shout it from the rooftops? My mother was Jennifer Lake, the third victim of The Player?"

Jake stood up and circled to the back of the couch. Folding his arms, he leaned against it. "You don't have to shout it out to anyone. You should've told me, and I think it would be of interest to the rest of the task force."

Kyra's mouth dropped open and prickles of fear raced across her skin. "I—I couldn't do that. Don't you do that. Don't you dare do that. Don't you dare tell anyone who I am."

Jake straightened up, his muscles coiled, nostrils flaring. "I wouldn't do that, but why? Why in God's name is it so important for you to keep your identity a secret from everyone?"

Kyra glanced over her shoulder at the sliding glass door that led to her little patio and whispered, "Because The Player is still out there…and he knows who I am."

Chapter Thirteen

Jake lunged forward, stopping inches away from Kyra, close enough to see the whiteness around her lips and the corner of her eye twitching. The cool, collected woman who seemed to float just above everyone else was rattled.

He clenched and unclenched his hands. "What does that mean, he knows who you are?"

"He knows his third victim left an eight-year-old daughter behind." She tossed her head, flicking back her thick ponytail. She took a deep breath and swallowed. "And we know he's still out there. He was never caught."

Jake knew backpedaling when he saw and heard it, and Kyra was pumping furiously. "Has The Player ever reached out to you?"

"N-no." She ran her hands over her face. "At least, not that I know of."

"You mean the playing card left by the dumpster out back?"

"That and..." She swept past him, grabbed her purse

from the divider where she'd dropped it and plunged her hand inside. "And this one."

She held up a red playing card, and he moved in to get a better look.

He snatched the queen of diamonds from her fingers and waved it in the air. "Is this what you found by your car today?"

"Yes." She retreated to the kitchen and hung on to the handle of the fridge. "Do you want something to drink? Beer? Water? Juice? Soda?"

The sheet of ice was coming down again, only this time he'd seen the cracks and knew where they were located.

He ignored her offer. "Why would you hide this from me, especially after the first one? There's no coincidence now, is there? Someone left these for you. Do you think it's The Player?"

"I was going to tell you about the second card." She poured herself a glass of orange juice and raised the carton. "Are you sure you don't want some? I don't have AC in this apartment and it's still warm from the Santa Anas, and you look…hot under the collar."

He ground his back teeth together and flicked the corner of the card. "You were going to tell me about the second card but not your connection to The Player."

"That's right." She leveled a gaze at him over the rim of her glass as she took a sip. "But you know that now, too."

He dropped back onto the couch, placing the card on the rough-hewn wood coffee table as if for a game of solitaire. He may as well have been playing solitaire for all the help Kyra was giving him.

"Do you think The Player left these as some kind of reminder or warning?"

"As if I need a reminder." She swirled the orange liquid in her glass. "As a warning? I thought you were convinced that The Player was not responsible for the killing spree we're witnessing now."

He tapped his finger on the card. "I was sure we had a copycat, but how would a copycat killer know about you? Especially with an identity change, how would some random person find you? In fact, how would The Player know you for Jennifer Lake's daughter?"

"There are a few people out there who know my identity. Quinn suggested it might be one of them."

"You told Quinn about this already?" He supposed he should feel happy that she was confiding in someone. He was sure Quinn was not advising her to keep this from the lead detective on the task force.

She set down her glass and faced him. "I tell Quinn everything."

"Quinn suggested someone other than The Player and The Copycat might be responsible for leaving the cards?"

"Matt Dugan."

"Who's Matt Dugan?"

"When my mom was murdered, I got shunted into the foster care system." Her whole body twitched. "A few of the families took in multiple foster kids for the money. Matt Dugan was one of those kids with a family the same time I was there."

"So, sort of like a foster brother."

Her full lips twisted into a bitter smile. "You could call him that. Like many kids in the system, Matt had issues. He liked starting fires, he liked hurting people and he liked me."

"Did he hurt you?" Talk about hot under the collar. A flash of heat claimed his chest and clawed its way up his throat. How could a system be so broken that it would put a vulnerable girl like Marilyn Lake in a home with disturbed youth?

"A few times before I caught onto him. Then I put him in his place." Her blue eyes flashed with a look he was sure never emanated from her mother's eyes.

Maybe Marilyn Lake hadn't been so vulnerable after all. "This Matt Dugan knows who you are?"

"He kept track of me. He stalked me and found out about my identity change. I suppose I should've made a clean break and moved to another state, but despite everything I never wanted to leave LA."

"Knowing about the current murders and how you might be feeling, is this something Matt would do?"

"Oh, yeah. He's one sick individual. Been in and out of the joint for everything from arson to robbery to domestic violence." She formed her fingers into a gun and pointed at him. "I keep track of him, too."

"Then maybe I need to pay Matt a visit."

"No!" She slammed her glass on the kitchen table. "That's not a good idea. I learned long ago, the best way to handle a stalker is to not handle him at all. He's looking for a reaction—any reaction. That's what fuels him. I never contact him. I don't acknowledge that I'm aware of his existence."

"Okay, okay." He peeled the card from the table. "I'm going to take this with me. I'm assuming there aren't going to be any prints, just like the other card, but you never know."

She strolled toward him from the kitchen and sat on the edge of the coffee table facing him, her nose almost touching his, her long lashes almost brushing his cheek. "Do I have your word you won't tell anyone on the task force who I am, not even Billy Crouch?"

"I won't tell anyone, but you have to promise to keep me in the loop. For God's sake, these cards could've been real clues to stopping this guy. That's what you want, isn't it? To stop this guy?"

"More than anything." She drew back from him and placed a hand over her heart. "I'll let you know if anything else pops up, and just so you know, Quinn never approved of my deception toward you."

"I didn't figure he did. He's not that kind of cop." Jake pushed up from the couch and picked up her water glass and untouched Scotch from the table. He separated himself from her by walking into the kitchen. If she got any closer to him, he'd promise her anything.

He placed the glasses in the sink. "Why didn't the court allow Quinn and Charlotte to adopt you? Why thrust you into the system when they had a couple who wanted you?"

She crossed one leg over the other and clasped her hands around her knee. "Because Quinn was an alcoholic."

Jake turned from the sink and gripped the edge of the counter behind him. "How would they even know that? I mean, a lot of cops are alcoholics. My dad was one of them."

She lifted and dropped her shoulders. "He told them. Quinn is honest...to a fault. He stopped drinking, went to AA, tried to do everything to convince them he and Charlotte would've been good parents. And they would've been. I can't tell you the number of times I ran to them when a foster care situation wasn't working out for me, which happened a lot."

"That's sad. Does he blame himself?"

"Of course he does. Most of all, he blames himself for not catching The Player." She held up the queen of diamonds. "You're taking this, right?"

Was that her way of kicking him out of her place?

"I am." He retrieved her empty juice glass from the kitchen table and added it to the others in the sink, just to buy more time with her. He'd discovered her secret and confronted her with it, and now she wanted him gone. He'd discovered more than her secret. He'd discovered layers to this woman that he'd never imagined.

She approached him and tucked the card in his shirt pocket, and then patted it. "There you go. I need to get some sleep."

"You're not afraid here by yourself? You said it. The Player is still out there."

"I know that." She reached past him for her purse on the table, unzipped the gun pouch and pulled out her weapon. "That's why I sleep with this by my side every night."

The gleam of the shiny metal piece in her hand matched the gleam in her eye, and something told him she'd rather sleep with that gun right now than any man—especially him.

KYRA SHOVED A box of tissues toward Desiree, who'd shared her story for the first time in the rape survivors support group. Kyra didn't have to say much. The other women and one man in the group had crowded around Desiree at the end of the meeting cooing words of encouragement and petting her.

The petite redhead blossomed under the attention.

Kyra raised her voice above the chatter. "I think we were all so excited to hear Desiree speak, we forgot something."

Tracy, the mother hen of the group, an upper-middle-class homemaker who'd been brutally assaulted and raped by the pool boy, flapped her arms. "Back in the circle, everyone."

People returned to the front of their chairs and joined hands. Tracy started the recitation and they all joined in. "We are not victims. We are survivors. We are not our pain. We rise above it."

Annika, the call girl who'd been beaten and raped by a john, raised her hands and said, "Amen, sistah."

Kyra repeated the amen in her own head. "See you all next week."

Kyra waited while everyone stacked their chairs in the corner. She and Candace held group sessions in the roomier outer office, locking the front door during those sessions. The groups ran themselves, and Kyra had never been more thankful for that than today with Jake's voice mail burning a hole in her phone.

After the last client left the office, Kyra pulled her phone out of the pocket of her sweater. She hesitated before tapping Play for the voice mail. If he was coming at her with more questions, she didn't want to listen. Last night she'd revealed way more than she'd ever intended.

She hit Play and Speaker, and held her breath as Jake's low voice rumbled over her phone. "Hello, Kyra. It's Jake. If you have time today, I'd like you to come with me to Melrose and meet Rachel. I'm heading over to do some follow-up on the video we watched yesterday. I just talked to Rachel, and she's having a hard time with the fact that a killer stole her phone to call in a dead body. I think the shock hit her last night. Let me know."

Kyra released her breath in a long stream. Work, not personal. And she could understand Rachel's uneasiness.

She returned Jake's call, and he answered from his car. "I wasn't sure you were available, so I'm on my way out there now."

"I was leading a group session. I'm heading out the door and can meet you at Rachel's work. Can you give me the address?"

He rattled off the address on Melrose Avenue in West Hollywood, all business now, the pity and even the anger stripped from his voice.

In a sick way, her status as the daughter of one of The Player's victims had given her bona fides in Jake's eyes to belong to the task force. She could've revealed it before to take a seat at the table, but she'd never used her mother's death to further her agenda and didn't intend to start now.

For all the freeways in LA, there was no easy access to West Hollywood from Santa Monica, and she sat in her car on Santa Monica Boulevard anxiously tapping her steering wheel in time to the music on the radio.

Forty-five minutes later, she rolled onto Melrose. Even on weekdays, the crowds surged onto this street, tourists and locals shopping, eating, gawking.

Hunting? Did this area have significance for the killer? Her gaze darted around the street, looking for a parking place—or a killer.

She spotted the store where Rachel worked and, a block down, zeroed in on a car pulling away from the curb across the street. She managed an illegal U-turn in the middle of the street and tucked into the space, careful not to bump the fenders of the high-end cars on either side.

She slid from the car and tugged her skirt down to her knees. She swiped her debit card into the parking meter and added time. The Santa Ana winds had dissipated, and with them the wildfire threat and the dry, suffocating heat, but the sun still beat down on the pavement, sending shimmering waves into the air that seemed to pulse with the traffic.

She strode to the corner to catch the signal because even if the LA County Sheriff's Department hadn't caught her making that U-turn, it didn't mean they wouldn't come down on her for jaywalking.

She joined the hustle and bustle of people as the signal changed and the little green man flashed. When she reached the other side, she noticed Jake's unmarked sedan parked in the red. Didn't the guy ever pay for parking?

She charged toward the store with the blue-and-gold awning and stepped inside. The man at the counter, helping another customer, sang out, "Be right with you."

No sign of Jake, but the low murmurs from the back of the store, behind the shivering beaded curtain, gave him away. She waved to get the clerk's attention, but when he didn't look her way she crept toward the rear and parted the strands of beads with two fingers.

Jake glanced up, a look of relief spreading across his face, as he sat across from a sobbing young woman with tats marching up one arm. Being a cop, he'd surely dealt with upset and traumatized people—it didn't mean he had to like it. The situation with Rachel probably confused him even more, as she'd been a rational human being yesterday. That was yesterday.

"Kyra's here." He gave up his seat and hovered by the chair that looked like it belonged in a dentist's office...or a torture chamber. "I told you she was coming. You can tell her everything you told me...and more."

Kyra took Rachel's trembling hand in both of hers. "Hi, Rachel. I'm Kyra. I just want to tell you, first off, how impressed I was by the help you gave the detectives yesterday. You kept your head, and you gave them valuable information."

Raising her tear-streaked face, black rivulets from

her eyeliner trailing down her cheeks, Rachel's voice cracked when she said, "I—I don't know what happened. I felt okay yesterday, a little creeped out but more mad than anything else. Then today when I came into work, it hit me. Some serial killer stole my phone. He saw my contacts, he knows my number, maybe he still has it."

Jake said, "If he does have it, he turned it off. More likely, he won't want to be caught with your phone in his possession so he tossed it."

"If it makes you feel any better, what you're experiencing is totally normal." Kyra patted Rachel's shoulder. "You were mad yesterday, maybe a little shocked. Today you've had time to digest what happened, and it *is* scary. But this guy stole your phone to use it, not to target or terrorize you. He's not interested in that and may not even know or remember who you are."

"You think so?" Rachel hiccupped.

"I do, but all that logic doesn't mean you still can't feel rattled." Kyra glanced around the back room, which obviously functioned as the piercing area. "Do you have a few minutes to talk right now, or do you have to go back to work?"

"I can talk for a few. Gustavo has me covered."

Kyra flicked her fingers at Jake. "Detective McAllister has some canvassing to do in this area."

"Yeah, that's right." Jake coughed and smacked his hand against the back of the chair. "I'm going to be retracing Rachel's steps from the other day if you want to catch up."

"I'll find you." Kyra scooted her chair closer to Rachel, their knees almost touching.

"Detective McAllister?" Rachel dabbed her face with the tissue Kyra handed to her. "Is this going to affect your recommendation for me as a dispatcher?"

"This?" Jake's eyebrows jumped to his hairline. "You mean your reaction to having a close encounter with a serial killer?"

Rachel nodded, shredding the tissue between her black-tipped fingernails.

"Absolutely not. We do like humans working in Dispatch." He winked and plunged through the beaded curtain, leaving it clacking and swaying behind him.

Rachel sat up straight and squared her shoulders. "I like Detective McAllister."

"So do I." Kyra plucked another tissue from the package in her purse and waved it at Rachel. "Now, tell me what you're feeling."

About fifteen minutes later, at the end of their mini-session, Rachel's cheeks were dry and she even managed a laugh. The haunted look in her eyes had disappeared, and a fiery light had replaced it. She'd definitely swung back to anger, and Kyra got a glimpse of the young woman who had so impressed Jake yesterday.

Kyra held out one of her cards between her fingers. "Call me anytime you like. My office is in Santa Monica, but I can meet you anywhere."

"Thank you." Rachel plucked the card from her fingers and dropped it in the front pocket of her polka-dot blouse, tied at the waist. She tugged on her earlobe.

"If you want another piercing for your ears, it's on the house."

"Thanks, Rachel." Kyra rose to her feet and smoothed her hands over her skirt. "I'm going to catch up with Detective McAllister. You let him know if you remember anything else, and you let me know if you're starting to feel panicked again."

"The sooner they catch this guy, the better." Rachel rubbed her arms. "Have the police identified that body from the Malibu fire?"

"Not yet."

"So, she's not like the other two, nobody reporting her missing. Nobody noticing her absence." Rachel launched from her seat and swept aside the curtain. "That's sad."

"Not yet. I'm sure law enforcement will get a hit soon."

"You know," Rachel said, aiming her gaze at the window across the store, "there are call girls on this block. They aren't as obvious as the ones on Hollywood Boulevard or Sunset, but they work it here. Maybe she was someone like that."

"Detective McAllister was right. You do have good instincts. I'm sure the task force is looking into all of that." She held out her hand. "You take care and don't hesitate to call me."

Rachel gripped her hand in a professional manner and dipped her chin. "I won't."

Kyra navigated her way through the cluttered store, stepped onto the sidewalk and looked both ways. What were they missing? Kelsey had gotten her nose pierced in this very store, and Rachel's phone had been stolen on this block. What was Marissa's connection to this area?

On her way to Uncommon Grounds, Kyra poked her head in at the pita place, looking for Jake's tall frame. He'd stand out, for his height and also the suit he wore on a warm, sunny Southern California afternoon.

Jake didn't dress to the nines like his partner did, but he had his own style that emphasized a casual masculinity. He didn't try too hard, but his clothes were well made and fit his muscular build to a T.

She puffed out a breath and made a beeline to the coffee place. When had she found the time to make such a detailed study of J-Mac and his sartorial splendor? Was it when he was waving her off crime scenes? Trying to get her kicked off task forces? Or when he was confronting her with truths about her past he'd ferreted out with snooping?

She barged through the front door of the coffee shop and nearly bowled over a woman carrying an Uncommon Grounds cardboard tray with four frothy drinks inserted in it.

"Sorry." Kyra held the door wide for the woman, who scowled at her anyway.

She spied Jake talking to an employee who looked like the manager. Jake was pointing to the corners of the store, probably trying to find more footage.

She waved, and he nodded. Then he shook the manager's hand and loped toward her.

"How's Rachel doing?"

"She's fine. I think the shock from yesterday wore

off, and the reality came at her like a freight train today." She tilted her head. "You did a good job reassuring her that the killer didn't have her in his sights. Do you believe that?"

"I do. Taking her phone was a crime of opportunity, which happened somewhere around here." He did a slow pivot to survey the four corners of the room.

Kyra jerked her thumb at the ceiling. "No more cameras with a better view of the store?"

"No. They're mostly geared to the counter to catch any funny business at the register or a robbery." He tipped his chin. "She did point out some regulars, and I wouldn't mind having a chat with a couple of the men who hang out here."

Her gaze tripped from one table to another, hosting mostly single people with their laptops stationed in front of them, stacks of papers, note cards, books and the occasional cup of coffee littering the tables. "What are all these people working on here?"

"My guess." Jake spread his hands. "Scripts, treatments, whatever you call them. This is LA, after all."

She nudged him. "C'mon, don't you think you have one good script in you from your experiences?"

His hazel eyes widened for a split second. "You really don't know, do you?"

"Know what?"

"I'll tell you over coffee." He leveled a finger at the counter. "Let's get a couple of those fancy drinks and sit outside to survey the scene for a while."

"You're on, but it's my treat this time. You got the pho yesterday."

"Was that just yesterday? Seems like a lifetime ago."

"Yeah, my lifetime." She put a hand on his arm as he fell in step with her. "I'll get the drinks. You nab a table."

"I'd rather get a first-hand look at what Rachel saw."

"Good point." They fell in line behind an older couple with matching gray braids down their backs.

Jake tipped his head to hers, his lips close to her ear. "Wanna bet they smoke weed and say things like namaste?"

She flattened her lips to contain the bubble of laughter that threatened to explode. "You shouldn't stereotype."

"Hell, that's part of the job. Isn't that part of your job? Don't you make assumptions about people when you first meet them?"

"Sure, I do, but a lot of times the therapy proves them to be false, and then I'm humbled. Aren't you ever humbled, Detective McAllister?"

"Often." He stepped to the counter and hunched forward to peer at the menu board on the wall.

"What can I get for you today?" The young man behind the counter smiled, which made his cheeks bunch up like apples.

He looked like a fish out of water among the other baristas and even some of the customers, with their piercings and tattoos and alternative hairstyles.

"Ma'am?"

Those apple cheeks flushed an appropriate red, and Kyra realized she was staring. "I'm sorry, yeah, I'll have a peach iced tea."

"And I'll have an ice coffee, plain. I'll add my own poison."

As the barista rang up the order, Kyra said, "You look like an escapee from another store."

"Ma'am?" A furrow formed between…Jordy's eyes.

"I just mean, you look too—" she leaned in and whispered "—clean-cut for this store."

He laughed. "It's not my regular store. I also work at one of our stores in Studio City."

"Not an aspiring actor, are you?"

"No, ma'am." He handed her a receipt. "Have a nice day."

They shuffled to the side to wait for their order, and Jake poked her in the ribs. "You just did it."

"Did what?"

"You stereotyped Jordy, the barista, because he didn't have tats or piercings. You didn't think he fit in with the West Hollywood crowd."

"And I was right."

"And I'm probably right about the braids."

"I wish spotting a killer was that easy." She sighed.

"Me, too." Jake rested an arm on the counter that lined up against the window with tall stools pulled up to it and USB ports in a row. "Rachel could've waited for her coffee here. She could've even plugged in her phone here to charge while she waited."

"And left it here." Kyra traced one of the ports with the tip of her finger. "Could've happened that way. She picked up her drink and forgot the phone."

"The killer saw it unattended and took his chance."

"This is a busy store." She nodded toward the door.

"One of the street cameras showed just how many people walked in and out of here."

"Could've been any one of them."

A barista called out from the pickup counter. "Order for Kyra."

Jake shouldered his way through the clutch of people waiting for their drinks and grabbed theirs. He handed her the tea and then followed her to the sugar station.

Jake dumped a couple of packets of sugar into his drink, while she opted for the fake stuff.

They wended their way to a table outside, drinks in hand, and sat across from each other in the shade of a Ficus tree, its roots buckling the sidewalk.

Kyra popped the lid off her tea and dumped in the sweetener. She swirled her straw in the amber liquid until all the white crystals disappeared and took one long sip before replacing the lid. "So, what don't I know about you, except just about everything?"

He shook his plastic cup, knocking the ice together. "You don't know that I already wrote a screenplay."

"What? No, you didn't."

"Do you remember the movie on Netflix called *Shots Fired*, starring Tito Valenti?"

"That wrestler?"

"The same. Did you see the movie?"

"I think I missed that one." She sipped her tea and raised her eyebrows. "That was you?"

"I wrote that screenplay and a second one called *Two Shots Fired*." He shrugged. "That one never got made, but they optioned it."

"I'm impressed. Did they pay you well?"

"Well enough to buy a house in the Hollywood Hills, not too far from here, actually."

"Super impressed." Why hadn't she heard that about him? Probably because she'd never asked. People knew she'd been working with Lizbeth at the time Lizbeth had double-crossed Jake and he'd gone after her in a rage. They probably figured she wouldn't want to hear anything about McAllister—nothing good, anyway. And she hadn't.

She toyed with her straw. "I will be waiting with bated breath for *Two Shots Fired*."

He coughed and wiped his eyes. "Don't wait too long. Tito could be a grandpa by then, all his muscles shriveled and sagging."

Her mouth quirked up on one side, her snappy comeback stalled on her lips as she took in the sight of an attractive young woman on her phone at another table. The woman looked up as a man on his phone approached, but she kept talking, smiling and laughing. When the man reached the table, she ended the call, as did he. They'd obviously been talking to each other.

He leaned forward, kissed her on the cheek and took the chair next to hers, not across, but next to.

"Hey, you." Jake tapped her plastic cup with his finger. "What's so fascinating over there when you have the screenwriter for *Shots Fired* sitting in front of you?"

"I was watching that couple at the table right next to the sidewalk." As Jake shifted his head, she said, "Don't be obvious."

"I'm a detective." He moved his chair, scraping it on the concrete. "Yeah? What about them?"

"Rachel told me that call girls work this block."

"They do."

"We, Rachel and I, were wondering about the woman found at the Malibu fire. You haven't ID'd her yet, right? No missing persons reports match her description?"

"I wouldn't say that. This is LA. It's a vast area and a lot of people go missing here—some on purpose, just like Marilyn Lake."

Her head snapped back. "Don't say that name in public."

"Sorry." He drew a line across his mouth with his fingertip. "We did consider the idea that the third victim—or she would've been the first victim—was a sex worker, but I don't think he's targeting prostitutes. If he swept her up in his net, it wasn't because he picked her up for business."

"No, but it could've been because she'd been frequenting this area. We already have one of the women tied to Melrose Avenue and the killer himself because of Rachel's phone."

"We'll ID her. Billy will." He took a sip of coffee. "I had the queen of diamonds fingerprinted and—just like her sister, the queen of hearts—it's clean. I also looked at the footage of the street in front of the station, taken yesterday when your car was parked there. A big, fat nothing again. If you had been in the lot, we would've gotten a look at the person who dropped that card next to your car. Couldn't catch anything on the street."

"I can guarantee you, if I'd parked my car in the

lot there wouldn't have been any card. Give the guy some credit."

"You're probably right." Jake caught a bead of moisture running down the outside of his cup and smeared it away. He picked up the cup and studied the blue logo on the side. "Uncommon Grounds. I've seen a lot of these popping up."

"I think it started in Portland. There are already a few in Santa Monica and once they get a foothold in Santa Monica and West Hollywood, you know they're going to take off."

He brought the cup closer to his face and traced over the zigzag on the logo that looked like mountains. "I've seen this before."

"Yeah, it's right behind you." She pointed over his shoulder at the same logo painted on the window of the store they'd just left.

"No, I mean I've seen this before." He grabbed the satchel at his feet and hauled it onto the table.

He unzipped it and dragged out a stack of files.

Kyra's heart skipped a beat. "You're not going to look at crime scene photos in the middle of a sidewalk patio, are you?"

"Not quite crime scene, but crime related." He glanced up. "Don't worry, nothing gruesome."

Her leg jiggled up and down, rocking the table. "What is it?"

"The car." He abandoned one file for another. "Pictures of the inside of Marissa's car."

Kyra hopped from her chair to the one next to Jake's and hovered over the open file on the table.

He flipped through the photos quickly until he stopped at one of a red compact. "This is Marissa's car. Just like with Kelsey's car, we found her phone and purse inside. Also, like Kelsey's car, there was no video of what occurred there when she was forced to abandon it."

He thumbed through the next few photos and snatched one from the pile. He stabbed his finger at the picture, and Kyra leaned in closer for a better view.

She jerked up her head. "It's a coffee cup—a coffee cup from Uncommon Grounds."

"You know how we were just discussing connections to this area?" His lids fell over his hazel eyes half-mast, and he seemed to be studying every face coming and going on the sidewalk from beneath them. "Looks like we might be right in the middle of his hunting ground."

Chapter Fourteen

Kyra craned her neck around to look at the coffee place behind them. "You think Marissa got her coffee at this Uncommon Grounds?"

"I know it could've been any of the other stores, but it's interesting, isn't it? Kelsey gets her nose pierced on this street. Rachel has her phone lifted on this street, most likely from Uncommon Grounds, and now Marissa is tied to this same area with an empty coffee cup in her car from the same place. It's a long shot, but we have to start somewhere and this seems like a good place to do that."

"I agree. What next?"

"As long as I'm here and as long as I have Marissa's picture with me, I'm going to ask that manager if she remembers Marissa. They must have their regulars."

"Should I go with you?"

"I'll go in alone." He rapped his knuckles on the table. "Save our spot."

Kyra's face fell just a little. As invaluable as she was to have on this task force, he already had a partner and he still didn't trust Kyra completely.

Jake returned to Uncommon Grounds with Marissa's picture in his pocket. When the manager saw him enter, he waved her over to the corner of the food display.

She stuffed a strand of brown hair beneath her cap. "Something else I can help you with, Detective?"

"You said you had regulars here." He whipped out the picture of Marissa. "Was she one of them?"

The manager gave the picture a hard look. "I don't think so. Pretty girl. Can I keep it?"

"The picture?"

"I want to show the staff. They'd know the regulars more than I would."

"Sure, you can keep it. You have my card. Let me know if anyone recognizes her."

Jake returned to the table outside and dropped into the uncomfortable metal chair. "That was a big nothing. She didn't recognize her, but I let her keep the picture and she's going to show the staff."

"Something might come of it." Kyra checked her phone. "I have an appointment. I'm also going to be talking to Marissa's friends later in a group chat. If anything comes up from that, I'll let you know. I'll definitely ask them about any connections Marissa had to this area."

"Thanks for your help with Rachel, and thanks for the coffee."

"I think you're right about her. She has good instincts and a calm demeanor. She'd work out great on Dispatch."

"I usually am right about people…most people." He stuffed the files back into his bag, wondering how many of them Kyra had gone through while he was inside. "Do you want me to walk you back to your car—in case you find any more cards?"

"I'm parked across the street, and with the number of cameras on this street I doubt I'll find any cards by my car." She stood up and tugged at her slim skirt, which hit just above the knees of her long legs. "I'll be sure to let you know if I do."

"Sure you will." He hitched the satchel over his shoulder and gave her a little salute. "Until next time."

She put on her sunglasses and nodded. Picking up his cup, she asked, "Done? There's a trash can on my way."

"Go for it." He watched her walk away, the sun glinting in the ponytail swaying against her back, which matched the gentle sway of her hips in the pencil skirt.

If Jennifer Lake possessed half the grace of her daughter, it's not surprising she thought she could make it in Hollywood.

Jake turned and strode back to his car on the other side of the street from Kyra's, keeping an eye on her as she walked. He stopped when she reached her car.

She disappeared for a second on the passenger side of the car and then popped up, waving her empty hands.

Grinning, he gave her a thumbs-up and proceeded to his own car. At least she knew he didn't trust her.

That sort of eased his conscience over what he planned to do next.

A FEW HOURS LATER, Jake logged off his laptop and snapped the lid. Matt Dugan had made it easy for Jake to find him because he was a dirtbag with a record a mile long—and he still lived in LA.

Billy swept into the task force headquarters, tossed a balled-up bag into the trash and called out, "Baller."

Jake snapped his fingers in the air. "Hey, baller, any luck tracking down which Uncommon Grounds Marissa's coffee cup came from?"

Billy pulled up a chair and collapsed in it, stretching his legs in front of him. "They don't track those serial numbers like that. Cups and other inventory travel between the stores so even if that cup was delivered to one store, there's nothing that says it stopped there and didn't travel to another store in the area."

"Gotcha." Jake rubbed his eyes. "Still no ID on the Malibu fire victim."

"Nope, and the alibi checked out for Kelsey's boyfriend, not that he was ever a prime candidate." Billy drew in his legs to make room for Jake. "You heading out?"

"Checking on a few leads."

"Mind if I sit these out?" Billy massaged the back of his neck. "I've got a headache coming on."

"Didn't expect you to join me." Jake swung his bag at his desk drawer. "I've got some ibuprofen in there if you need it."

"I've got my own stash. Hey, you're not going to see our task force therapist, are you?"

"No, I told you I saw her earlier when Rachel Blackburn needed some help."

"And did you happen to ask her about her friend, the TV reporter, for me?"

"What are you, in middle school? If you want to ask her out, do it. Do you need her friend to send her a note letting her know you like her?"

"A little introduction to smooth the way never hurt. You need to venture away from your blow-up doll now and then to see how it works in the real world."

A few cops laughed as Jake threw a pen at Billy. He didn't have a blow-up doll, but it had been a while since he'd had a real date. He'd dipped a toe in the online dating scene but had heard too many stories about scams and misrepresentations to be comfortable in that world.

Besides, who wanted to date a guy with trust issues?

Armed with information from Matt Dugan's parole officer about his last known residence, Jake got behind the wheel of his Crown Vic and plugged the address into his GPS.

He knew the area, the shady side of Van Nuys.

The only problem with a sneak attack was that Dugan might not be home, but Jake didn't want to give him a chance to concoct some story—or to contact Kyra.

Once off the freeway, Jake tooled down Van Nuys Boulevard, past the car dealerships, the free clinics, the methadone treatment centers, the churches and the working girls getting a jump on the competition. His GPS directed him to turn left at the next light.

After his turn, he slowed to crawl along the block, stucco apartment buildings in various hues standing rainbow sentry on either side of the street. He spotted Dugan's place, a grimy yellow building going for a Spanish hacienda look that fell short with its chipped stucco, missing red roof tiles and battered arched entry leading to a messy courtyard containing a broken-down barbecue, a few dead potted plants and a unicycle.

He parked and exited the vehicle, staring hard at a clutch of men lounging on the steps of the apartment building next to Dugan's. He grabbed his jacket from the back seat of the car and put it on slowly to give the vatos sizing him up a look at the weapon in his shoulder holster.

As he made his way to the yellow building, the guys meandered away in different directions. Probably parolees holding drugs or weapons or warrants. As he passed beneath the yellow arch, a baby wailed from one of the apartments and a man let loose with a sneeze from another. You'd be hard-pressed to keep anything a secret from your neighbors here.

A quick glance at the dull metal numbers affixed to the right of each front door led Jake upstairs to number twelve. He knocked and stood slightly to the side of the door but in clear view of the peephole. Shuffling sounds came from the other side of the paper-thin door, and Jake's muscles tensed.

"Who is it?" A male voice, ragged from cigarettes and booze, boomed through the open window with the sagging screen to the left of the door.

"You're in luck, Dugan. It's not your parole officer. LAPD Homicide, open the door." Jake banged his fist against it for good measure.

The door swung open, and a big man with a shaved

head and a goatee loomed in the space. "Homicide? You bastards haven't framed me for that one, yet."

"The day is young, Dugan. Let me in." Jake didn't wait for the invite and pushed past him, stepping into a cluttered space with the skunky scent of weed hanging over it. He sniffed the air.

"It's legal in homes." Dugan waved at the bong on the coffee table. "And medicinal."

"I don't care about that. Did I say I was Vice?" Jake squinted at the deck of playing cards on the battered coffee table. He *did* care about that.

"Then what do you want, Mr. Homicide?" Dugan folded his pumped-up arms over his chest, and a vein stood out on his neck beneath the tattoo of letters curling into an AB, which proclaimed Dugan a member of the Aryan Brotherhood.

This was the guy stalking Kyra? No wonder she carried a gun.

"Do you know Kyra Chase?"

A smile that didn't have anything do to with happiness spread across Dugan's face, and a knot formed in Jake's gut.

"Why? Is she dead…like her momma?"

A muscle ticked in Jake's jaw, but he matched Dugan smile for smile. "C'mon, Dugan. You'd know that wasn't true because I hear you keep close tabs on her."

"She wishes, my man. You know them bitches." Dugan stroked his goatee. "They don't never forget their first."

A white-hot rage zipped through Jake's veins. If Dugan had been Kyra's first, it had been by force.

"You obviously know who she is." Jake widened his stance and dug the heels of his shoes into the stained carpet. "Have you been by her place? Her car?"

"Nope. Did she send you here?" Dugan ran his nails along his arm like a junkie looking for a fix. Weed didn't do that.

"No. She doesn't know I'm here." Jake wandered over to the table and swept up the cards.

"Hey, I was playing that game." Dugan took a step forward, and Jake stopped him with a look.

He shuffled the cards in his hands. "You've heard about this serial killer who's copying the MO of the same killer that murdered Kyra's mother, haven't you?"

"I don't pay much attention to that stuff." Dugan's gaze tracked every flick of Jake's fingers as he plucked two cards from the deck.

He held up the two dark queens. "Looks like you haven't been playing with a full deck, Dugan."

He licked his lips. "What do you mean?"

"You're missing the queen of hearts and the queen of diamonds." Jake tossed the deck back onto the table, where it fanned out.

"So what? That's some old deck someone left here." He clenched his ham fists at his sides. "I didn't have nothing to do with no murders."

"Maybe not, but you did have something to do with terrorizing Kyra Chase." Jake rushed the big man and rammed him up against the thin wall, which quaked under their combined weight.

Jake squeezed his hand against the beefy neck, his fingers pinching into the Aryan Brotherhood tattoo.

"I'm here to tell you to stop, or you're gonna wind up back in the slammer faster than you can say three strikes. You got that?"

Dugan gurgled in response and Jake took it as a yes. He released Dugan, and he slid down the wall, choking and clawing at his chest.

"And since this is a faulty deck, I'll just take it with me." He gathered the cards and put the stack in his pocket. "Learn to play solitaire on the computer."

Jake strode from the apartment, leaving the door open on Dugan's gasping sounds. The guy deserved worse for tormenting Kyra. At least the killer himself didn't have Kyra in his sights. Why would he? He wouldn't have access to the original case files on The Player and even if he did, you'd have to know what you were looking for to make the connection between Marilyn Lake and Kyra Chase.

Should he tell Kyra he'd paid a visit to Dugan and cleared things up? He yanked open his car door, shrugged out of his jacket and tossed it in the back. She probably wouldn't appreciate his efforts. Instead of the white knight, he'd come across looking like the frog.

He raced back to the station to make his own four-thirty briefing. He wanted to give everyone a heads-up on the Melrose connection between Kelsey, Rachel's phone and Marissa's cup from the coffee place in the same area.

When he walked into the task force war room, his gaze tracked to Kyra chatting with Brandon. She lifted her eyebrows at him, and he nodded her way, a sense of relief flooding his system. He'd spared her from any more random cards showing up on her doorstep. He didn't even need to take the credit for it.

He grabbed a file from his desk and signaled to Brandon to follow him to the briefing room to start the slideshow. When everyone was gathered, Jake presented the Melrose info, calling out the two sheriff's deputies from the West Hollywood division on loan to the task force to help canvass that area. Then he turned the meeting over to Billy for an overview of their efforts in identifying the Malibu fire victim.

Jake wound up the meeting by asking for any new information or clues. One of the detectives who was working closely with the medical examiner's office confirmed that both Marissa and Kelsey had small puncture wounds in their necks, which may have been how the killer had gotten the women away from their cars and into his without much of an apparent struggle. Both toxicology tests were pending. Jake assured everyone once the drug used to subdue the women was identified it would give them another avenue to check.

"This guy is not as clean as he thinks he is." He signaled Brandon to bring up the last slide, which contained pictures of the three murder victims. They had to remember the stakes here. "Anything else?"

From the back of the room, Kyra's hand shot up and uneasiness stirred in his gut, which was reason number eighty-eight why you didn't get involved with anyone from work. "Ms. Chase? You have something to add?"

Her voice, confident and composed, rang out. "I had an extensive conversation with Marissa Perez's friends this afternoon over the phone, and I wanted to bring up the issue of the jewelry and Kelsey's missing nose stud."

She commanded the attention of the room with her cool, professional demeanor, and a little flicker of pride tapped his chest, although he didn't know why or at least didn't want to look at it too closely. "Go ahead."

"Marissa's friends told me she always wore a jade bracelet. I don't know if that was found on her and the friends don't, either, as her belongings are still in evidence. I wanted to know if the jade bracelet was found with Marissa."

Jake turned to his partner. "Billy?"

"I don't remember." Billy pointed a finger at Brandon. "Can you find and bring up the photo of Marissa's possessions?"

Brandon turned off the connection from the computer to the display and began clicking through the electronic files on Marissa's case.

Brandon murmured to nobody in particular. "Got the files. Clothing, jewelry. Here."

He reactivated the display and a photo of jewelry appeared on the screen.

Jake said, "Zoom, please."

The image of the pieces got bigger and contained a pair of hoop earrings, two necklaces—one with a cross, the other with the letter *M*, and three rings.

"I don't see a bracelet. Anyone see a bracelet?" Jake glanced around the room. "So, Marissa wasn't found with a jade bracelet her friends say she wore all the time and Kelsey didn't have her nose stud, which her parents said she'd just gotten. Either those pieces were lost in the struggle, at the dump sites or our boy is taking something other than his victims' fingers for his trophy. To be sure Marissa didn't just leave it at home that day, I'll reach out to her roommate again."

Kyra coughed and Jake jerked his head up. "Anything else, Ms. Chase?"

"Uh, no." She stepped back to her place against the wall.

"Lights." Jake waved an arm in the air. "Thanks, everyone. Good work. We'll get this guy. I can feel it."

The team members who had desks in the war room shuffled back to their seats, the rest left for their own desks or left for the day.

As Jake pulled up a chair to his own desk, Kyra sauntered over and leaned her hip against the corner. "I did have something to add at the end, but I didn't want to announce it."

"Oh?" Jake's pulse ticked up a few notches. He couldn't help it. Excitement and drama seemed to swirl around this woman, and it drew him into her orbit every time.

"Marissa's roommate, Darcy, was on the call today and she invited me over to their place tomorrow—not only to look for the bracelet but to talk with her. She's still pretty upset."

"Can't Darcy just look for the bracelet herself? That's what I was going to ask her to do."

"Darcy is staying with friends right now. She can't go back to the apartment."

"Understood. Thanks for letting me know." His cell

phone, sitting on the desk next to his computer, buzzed with an incoming text.

Kyra glanced down at it and then at his face. "Do you need to get that?"

"It's just a text, not a call." He drummed his fingers on the desk. "Is there anything else?"

"No." She picked up his phone and handed it to him, and then pushed away from the desk with her hip.

He looked down at the display and a text from Mike's Bike Shop. He tapped it, and he scanned the message from Matt Dugan.

I left those cards but someone paid me. if you wanna know who and u want the 411 on Mimi, I take cash

KYRA SLIPPED THE set of keys to one of the LAPD detective squad sedans into the pocket of her jacket, which she usually wore in the chilly AC of the station. She caught her breath as one of the guys from the task force swept up behind her to drop off the keys to a squad car.

He smiled and said, "You're a good addition to the task force. Glad to have you on board. Have a nice evening."

"Thanks. You, too." Her fingers curled around the keys so tightly they pinched her fingers.

She had to be ready for Jake's exit. Would he go straight to his meeting with Matt? She hoped so.

Hearing voices from the war room, she ducked into the lunchroom and flattened herself against the wall.

Jake's voice carried down the hallway. "I don't have any plans tonight. Grab some dinner on the way home."

A voice that sounded like Billy's murmured something in reply.

Jake swore. "Dude, if you want to meet Megan Wright, ask Kyra yourself or just call the TV station. When has the lack of an introduction ever fazed you before?"

Kyra pressed her fingers to her lips. Billy wanted to meet Megan? Seemed there was a lot Jake McAllister was keeping from her. A whole helluva lot.

She couldn't try to follow him on foot out to the parking lot. He'd make her in two seconds. She had to believe the noises from the other room meant he was leaving.

Lowering her head and counting the number of tiles on the floor, she scurried from the station and walked quickly to the unmarked cars in the lot. The car she wanted wasn't even locked, so she slid behind the wheel and slumped down. She had no doubt if the LAPD wanted to find out who'd taken one of their unmarked detective cars after the shift change they'd have no problem seeing her on camera, but she'd worry about that later.

She watched the comings and goings over the rim of the steering wheel until she saw Jake's unmistakable stride in the parking lot.

He opened the trunk and loaded his satchel, which contained his laptop, and a couple of boxes of files. Then he climbed into the driver's side and took off.

Kyra started the car and pulled out of the parking lot after him. He wouldn't be expecting one of the other detectives to follow him, but she stayed a few car lengths behind him.

When Jake turned onto a crowded Sunset Boulevard, her stomach knotted. He was going home—and she had his address. Had he already talked to Matt over the phone? No, she'd watched him too closely. After the initial message from Matt, he'd texted a few times and then seemed to settle in to work.

She'd known that the text on Jake's phone had come from Matt. She recognized Mike's Bike Shop as the motorcycle repair place where Matt worked. She couldn't imagine Matt reaching out to a cop. Jake must've contacted Matt first.

So, did she feel sorry about borrowing an LAPD vehicle and following Jake? Not at all. He already knew her car and would've spotted the tail.

She could call Matt and ask him what he was doing, but then she'd be in his debt. And she never, ever wanted to be in Matt Dugan's debt. Besides, she couldn't trust a word out of Matt's mouth. She couldn't trust a word out of Jake's mouth, either.

When he turned off the boulevard and started heading for the hills, she slowed the car. She couldn't follow him to his house in the Hollywood Hills with the winding, narrow roads and spaced-apart housing. He'd see her headlights behind him at every turn.

After the first mile into the hills and as other cars dropped off, Kyra pulled into a turnout that led to a small dog park. She cut her lights and buzzed down the window.

Matt would most likely meet Jake at the bike shop. That's where Matt conducted all his business, and this was business. He wouldn't have Jake at his apartment—too risky with the drugs and weapons and unsavory friends. She pulled up the GPS on her phone. She knew the exact locations of the bike shop and Matt's apartment. She believed in keeping her enemies close, or at least on her radar.

If Jake was driving to Van Nuys, and she believed he was, he'd have to wend his way down the hill again and take Sunset. He'd have to pass this way and she'd see him.

Her stomach rumbled and she regretted not eating something at the station while she waited for Jake to leave. Of course, she could have this all wrong. Maybe Matt had already said all he had to say to Jake over text messaging. Maybe they'd set up their meeting for another night.

But she knew the way Matt's mind worked. If he had info to sell Jake, he'd want to do that right away. She'd have to get to Matt before Jake did. She could convince Matt that Jake wanted to entrap him, to arrest him and send him back inside.

Each time a pair of headlights came winding down the hill, Kyra's heart jumped, until about an hour into her wait when she spotted Jake's sedan. Of course, he'd use his police car. He was technically on police business.

When the red of his taillights disappeared around

the next bend, Kyra pulled out of her hiding place and hurtled down to Sunset.

She saw Jake's car make the left turn. He had to be going to Van Nuys. She'd take the risk. If she couldn't beat Jake to his destination, there was no point in showing up at all.

When she hit the signal at Sunset, she flicked on the light inside the car and squealed around the corner. She'd been in Quinn's car enough times to know how things worked.

She floored it and blared the siren a few times to get around traffic. Jake wouldn't wonder at an unmarked car racing to a call, even if he noticed it. Other cars parted for her as she careened down Sunset, leaving Jake in her dust.

If Mike's wasn't their meeting place, she'd find out soon enough. And if it was, she'd catch Matt by surprise and convince him Jake was up to no good. What *was* Jake up to?

She cranked up her speed on the freeway, slipping into the carpool lane, the red light still revolving in the window of the car. When she got off the freeway, she continued pressing her luck on Van Nuys Boulevard. She'd passed only two patrol cars on her way, and neither one had seemed interested in her pursuit, probably because nothing had come over their radios.

She finally cut off the light and stopped bleeping the siren within about two blocks of Mike's. She'd gotten a good head start on Jake, but she'd have to act quickly.

She spotted the yellow sign with the motorcycle on

it and cruised past the closed metal doors of the shop. She knew the owner had a patio in the back of the shop on the alley where bikers gathered sometimes, smoked a little weed and harassed the working girls. Matt's unofficial office. She knew a lot more about her former foster brother than she'd ever let on to him.

She wheeled the big car around the corner and parked it alongside the curb. Before she got out of the car, she hitched her purse across her body with the gun pouch facing out. She scrambled from the car, ignoring a homeless guy and a couple in the shadows, their heads together with their drug dealer.

She stepped into the alley, her nose twitching at the smell of garbage. She still had her work clothes on, and her heels clicked too loudly on the asphalt.

A yellow light spilled onto the white picket fence that marked the patio behind Mike's. As she approached, Kyra called out softly. "Matt? Matt, it's Mimi."

If she had to deal with any of the guys from the shop, she'd try to scare them off too with the promise of an LAPD cop on his way to wreck their little party.

But there was no party. She saw no heads poking above the fence, and she cursed under her breath. She'd been wrong. Jake could be meeting with Matt right now, and Matt could be telling him all kinds of things…about her.

Her ears picked up a slow moan that made the hair on the back of her neck quiver. She flattened her hand against her gun pouch. "Matt?"

When she reached the fence and peered over, she

staggered back. Matt Dugan, her nemesis, lay sprawled on the patio, foam bubbling at the side of his mouth and his eyes rolled back in his head. Was he dead?

And then he moaned again.

Chapter Fifteen

Jake rolled down Van Nuys Boulevard just in time to witness the underbelly come alive as the sun sank in a hazy sky.

Dugan had set up their meeting behind his place of work, a motorcycle repair shop that had closed a few hours ago. He'd indicated he conducted all his business from a small patio in the back of the shop. Jake was sure that business could result in several arrests. But he had a different mission.

He parked in front of the business and loped around to the back. A couple veered out of his way by crossing to the other side of the street, the male partner tugging the rim of his baseball cap lower on his face. Maybe they'd just come from doing business with Dugan.

Jake followed the building around the back and spotted an area enclosed by a white picket fence—kind of homey for an alley.

As he peered over the slats, his heart slammed against his chest. The door to the patio stood ajar, sagging on one hinge, and he barreled through it toward the man sprawled on the ground, a woman hovering over him.

Then the woman turned, and Jake almost doubled over from the sock to his belly.

"Kyra, what are you doing here? What's wrong with him?"

Her blue eyes shimmered like waves in a pool. "I think it's a drug overdose. He was conscious when I got here, but he's out now. His pulse is weak. Do you have any Narcan on you?"

"If I were Vice, maybe." He crouched beside her, nudging her away from the fallen man. He placed his fingers against Dugan's neck and rolled him onto his side. "Have you called 911?"

"Not yet. I just found him."

A whisper of...something flitted across the back of his neck.

"C-can you do it? I don't want to have to explain my presence here." She pressed her hand against her heart. "I swear, he was like this when I found him. I'll explain everything to you."

Jake already had his phone out and was calling 911. Before he even started talking to the 911 operator, Kyra scrambled to her feet and fled from the patio and the dying man—her foster brother.

Jake gave his location to the 911 operator and dropped his phone on the ground. He bent his head, putting his face close to Dugan's. "Don't bail on me now, you SOB. Who hired you to plant those cards? Who was it? Give me a name."

Dugan was fading fast and probably couldn't even

hear him. He kept trying anyway, grabbing on to Dugan's hand. "Can you hear me? Squeeze my hand for yes."

A breath that sounded like a death knell rattled in Dugan's chest.

"Did the killer pay you to leave the cards?"

Dugan's rough hand lay limply in his own.

Sirens filled the alley and vehicles screeched to a stop, but Jake kept hold of Dugan's hand.

He tried again. "Was it The Player?"

Dugan sputtered, and he convulsively squeezed Jake's hand.

"Drug overdose?" The EMTs swarmed onto the patio, and Jake grabbed the slats of the fence to pull himself up and out of their way.

"Looks like it." Jake flashed his badge. "He's an informant. We had a meeting, and... I found him like this."

Jake stepped over the fence while the EMTs started working on Dugan. An officer from the Van Nuys division intercepted him.

"Do you know this man's identity?"

"Matthew Dugan. He's a parolee. Works in the shop. We had a meeting. He was going to give me some info on a case I'm working—The Copycat Player."

"Oh, damn." The officer shook his head. "I hope you got your information out of him before the dope kicked in."

"I didn't, so I'm hoping like hell those guys can save him, but it doesn't look good. His pulse was weak."

"They'll do what they can." As a small crowd of

people gathered in the alley, the cop took some more information from Jake.

Jake stayed until the EMTs loaded Dugan into the ambulance. They hadn't declared him dead yet, no sheet over his head, still connected to an IV.

As the doors closed on Dugan, Jake fished a card from his pocket and handed it to the officer. "Let me know if he comes back like Lazarus. I'd really like to get my info from him."

"Will do."

The clutch of looky-loos began to scatter as Jake made his way back to his car. When he got behind the wheel, he clenched it, along with his jaw. What the hell had just happened?

How had Kyra known about his meeting with Dugan? Had her former foster brother called to warn her? Maybe he threatened to blackmail her, and she came out here to pay up before Jake got there.

How had she paid him? In drugs? What was she doing over his body? Why hadn't she called 911? She must've been waiting a long time for Dugan to exit her life. If he'd been stalking her and could be paid off to terrorize her with those cards, she wouldn't shed any tears over his death. But being happy someone was out of the picture was a far cry from helping him along.

He released the steering wheel and rolled his shoulders. Then he retrieved his cell phone and called Kyra.

It rang once before her husky voice poured into his ear. "Is he alive?"

"He looked like it when they loaded him in the ambulance."

She let out a breath. "He always did have problems with drugs."

"We need to meet. I wanna know what you were doing there."

"I'm waiting for you now."

"Where?"

"In front of your house."

Great. Had he ever given her his address? The woman probably had access to a lot more information than he could dream of. "Wait there. I'm on my way."

He negotiated his way back to the freeway, which was a lot less crowded than on his journey to see Dugan. In less than forty minutes, he was turning off Sunset and snaking his way to his oasis.

He pulled into the drive that led to his house and jammed on his brakes when he saw the unmarked LAPD detective car in front of his place. When Kyra stuck one long leg out of the car, he murmured. "Son of a…"

He slammed his car door and locked it. Couldn't be too careful around her.

"Did you steal that car from the station?"

She glanced behind her as if she'd forgotten how she got here. "Borrowed. I'll return it tonight."

"They'll have you on camera."

She shrugged. "Only if someone's looking for it. Nobody will be looking for it. The detective in Juvenile brings in his own car."

"You know just enough to be dangerous." He stalked past her to his front porch. "How'd you find out where I live?"

Her eyes widened. "You told me."

"I didn't give you my address. There are a lot of homes in the Hollywood Hills."

"Billy told me."

"How'd you…?" He turned at the front door, gripping the door handle. "Never mind."

He pushed open the door and stood aside, gesturing her across the threshold with a sweep of his arm.

The gesture was wasted on her. She stood on the porch, eyes closed, nostrils flared. "It's beautiful here. Peaceful. You don't even feel like you're in the city."

It *was* peaceful. "I call it my oasis."

Her eyelids flew open, and she stepped past him into the entryway. How did she still manage to smell like roses and sunlight after a long day of work, stealing a police vehicle and finding a dying man?

He pointed to the most uncomfortable chair in the house. "Sit and start talking."

She saw through the ruse and sank onto the sofa, the soft leather whispering beneath her weight. "Can I have something to drink first? I'm parched. Water is okay."

He dropped his bag by the front door and marched into the kitchen. He got her the water and grabbed a bottle of beer for himself, although he had a feeling he needed to be the clearheaded one here.

She took the glass from him with a thanks and downed half of it before he'd even sat down in the chair across from her.

Just like in any interrogation, he didn't want her getting too comfortable. "How did you know about my meeting with Dugan?"

"Did he call you first?" She skimmed her long, delicate fingers along the outside of the glass. "No, he'd never call a cop. You contacted him first. Why?"

He took a gulp of beer to tamp down his anger, knowing full well alcohol was no answer to fury. "That's not how this works. Answer my question."

A little smile lifted the corner of her mouth. "I saw his text on your phone at the station. I recognized the sender—Mike's Bike Shop. I know that's where Matt worked...works. I'd just mentioned Matt to you last night, so I didn't think it was some coincidence. Quinn told me there are no coincidences."

Damn Roger Quinn. Did he realize he'd created a monster?

"I did one better than just contact Dugan—I met the lowlife this afternoon."

A flare of petty pleasure burned in his belly when he saw the smile fall from her lips and her cheeks pale.

"You met with Matt today?"

"I did."

"Why?"

"I wanted to know if he was the one who planted those cards for you."

"And was he?"

"Yes."

She dropped her chin to her chest and tapped the tips of her fingers together. "I see. It doesn't surprise me. So, why the follow-up meeting?"

"When he sent me that text, he promised to tell me who paid him to leave the cards."

Her head jerked up. "Someone paid him to do it?"

"That's what he said in his text." Jake lifted one shoulder. "If he doesn't come out of his overdose, we'll never know."

"Let me guess." She swirled her water in the glass. "He was going to tell you for a price."

"Of course."

"He could've been lying to you."

"Maybe. Hopefully, I'll find out." She opened her mouth and he raised his finger. "My turn. How'd you know the time and place of our meeting? You may have seen the first line or two of that text, but you didn't read the whole thing or the follow-ups."

"That's where the theft of the car comes in." She took a dainty sip of the water as if to counter her confession. "I figured you'd spot me if I followed you in my own car, so I did the deed in a nondescript sedan, one you'd hardly notice even if you were looking for a tail...and you weren't."

He set his bottle on the table next to him harder than he meant to. The crack made her jump. *Good.* "You did not follow me all the way to my house and then to Van Nuys, reaching the bike shop before I did, all without my noticing you."

She folded her hands in her lap on top of her skirt. "I figured you'd be meeting at Mike's because I know that's where Matt works and does his dirty deeds. I just didn't know the time, and I didn't want to sit on Van Nuys until midnight. I followed you halfway up the hill and waited in a turnout until I saw you come down the hill."

"How'd you beat me to the meeting place?" A

prickle of suspicion teased his brain, and he held up his hands. "Wait, stop. I don't want to know."

"I was driving an unmarked LAPD sedan." She cocked one eyebrow. "I'm sure you can figure it out."

"Yeah, that I can figure out, although I can't believe your...nerve." He gripped the neck of his bottle. "What I can't figure out is why. Why did you need to get there before me? Why was it so important for you to talk to Dugan before I did? Or stop him talking to me."

"If Matt's lips are moving, chances are he's lying. I didn't want him to tell you a bunch of lies about me, and he would have."

"Who said he was going to talk about you? He was going to tell me who paid him to plant those cards." He watched her face closely.

Sensing his scrutiny, she raised the glass to her lips to hide the bottom portion of her face. "Matt was obsessed with me. He wouldn't miss a chance to talk about me, spread lies. You don't even know that someone paid him to leave the cards. He'd tell you anything to collect a little dough. He has a problem with drugs—in case you didn't notice."

"Why not just tell me that, then? Why go to all the trouble of stealing a car and following me?"

She widened her eyes. "Maybe if you'd told me you'd contacted him from the beginning. Why did you sneak around behind my back to find Matt?"

Jake jumped up from the chair. He didn't appreciate being in the hot seat in his own home during what was supposed to be his own interrogation. "I did it for you."

She dropped her lashes over her eyes, closing herself off even more. "Interesting take."

"When you told me you suspected Matt of leaving the cards, I wanted to make sure he stopped. I wanted him to leave you alone."

"Sweet, but I've been handling Matt Dugan most of my life." She leaned back on the couch and wedged her feet against the coffee table. "And you thought you did a good deed because he admitted to playing tricks with the cards, which he may or may not have done."

"Oh, I'm sure he did it."

"Because of your super-awesome detective skills?"

"Because—" he yanked his suit jacket from a stool at the kitchen counter where he'd left it when he came home from work and dipped his hand in the pocket "—I found these at that dump he calls an apartment."

As he spread out the playing cards in his hands, Kyra shot up straight. "He had a deck of cards in his house? So what?"

"A deck of cards that was missing two queens. You wanna guess which ones?"

"That bastard. He *did* do it." Her eyes glittered, and Jake had to wonder who had more to fear in the ongoing skirmish between Matt and Kyra.

"He didn't even admit it to me at the time, but I knew. So, I took the cards. Then he contacted me later to let me know he'd give up the person who paid him to do it...for a price. It could lead to something in this case if he does. If he survives."

"Then I hope he does." She downed the rest of the water and sauntered to the kitchen to put the empty glass in the sink. She pointed to a framed photo on the counter. "Who's that?"

"That's my daughter, Fiona."

Kyra's lips formed an O. "She's cute. I didn't know you had a daughter. Didn't know you had a wife."

"Once upon a time before we got divorced."

Several emotions played across Kyra's face at once, ending with a furrowed brow. "Does your daughter stay with your ex?"

"She does. In Monterey. My ex remarried." He schooled the bitterness from his voice before he continued. "She married one of the partners in her law firm and he relocated up there, so she took Fiona and moved."

"You didn't have any say in it?"

"I approved of it." He tossed back the rest of the beer, but it couldn't douse the bitterness this time. "I was a lousy father, anyway."

"You mean you were a busy father." She planted her hands on the granite counter and hunched forward. "I doubt you were a lousy father any more than Quinn would've been a lousy father."

He met her eyes; the iciness had melted into pools of soothing balm. Was this the way she looked at her clients to assure them they weren't losers who needed some stranger to talk with to sort out their sorry lives?

He grunted. "Why do you care?"

"Maybe I'm just trying to apologize for causing you so much grief tonight even though it would've had the same outcome whether I'd intervened or not. You would've found Matt in the same condition I did."

He scraped the soggy blue foil label from his bottle with his fingernail.

Kyra sucked in a breath. "You're kidding me."

He glanced up from his task. "What?"

"You think I had something to do with Matt's overdose?"

Did he?

"Of course not. Did I say that?"

"Sometimes you don't have to say anything at all. If you have super-awesome detective skills, I have super-awesome therapist skills."

He abandoned his project, picked up the bottle and dropped it in the recycling bin, Kyra's eyes following his every move.

"I don't think you killed Matt Dugan."

"You think I delayed calling 911."

He planted himself in front of her and squared his shoulders. "Who could blame you?" Her lashes fluttered and a rose blush stole across her cheeks. The spark hadn't hit her eyes though, so he hadn't stirred her ire. Was she flustered at his closeness?

He could reach for her right now and angle his mouth across hers, plunge his fingers in the silky strands of her hair, free it from the ponytail that kept it and her under tight control.

She blinked several times and stepped back. "I can assure you, I did not delay calling 911. When you arrived, I had just gotten there."

"Then I believe you."

She wiped her palms on her skirt. "I'd better take that car back to the station before someone misses it."

"Good idea."

"You're not going to…?"

"I'm not going to rat you out." He skirted around her to leave the kitchen. "You may not have known about my wife and child, but you do know I'm someone who doesn't always play by the rules, don't you? You'd know that about someone before joining forces with him, wouldn't you?"

"You make me sound…calculating. You know why I wanted on the task force. The fact that I had to work with you worried me until I got to know you better. You're a good cop with good instincts."

"Who doesn't always play by the rules."

She winked. "That's just a bonus."

"I'm going to call the hospital later to check on Matt. Do you want me to keep you posted?"

"Of course. I hope you get what you want out of him." She picked up her purse from the couch cushion. "Thanks for taking charge back there."

Had he taken charge? It seemed as if she'd been in control from the moment she'd seen the text on his phone.

"Be careful driving down the hill. There aren't many lights. And don't do anything stupid with that car."

"Yes, sir." She touched her fingers to her forehead. "Let me know what happens with Matt."

"I will." He moved past her to open the front door, and the air between them hung heavy with expectation. He wanted something more from her. He wanted her to tell him the whole truth. What had Matt been about to reveal about her? Why couldn't she trust him?

A little voice whispered in his ear. *Because you went behind her back to track down Matt Dugan.*

Stepping onto the porch, she lifted her hand. "You have a very cool house, by the way. *Shots Fired* really paid off."

He watched her get into the car and pull out of his driveway. While standing outside, he made a call to the hospital and a nurse told him Dugan was still in a coma. That didn't sound good.

He returned inside and picked up the picture of his daughter. He really wanted to see her right now, but he and Tess had agreed that Fiona didn't need to be here when he was working a big case, especially a task force like this one.

Had he been a good father to Fiona? Probably the best dad move he'd made was giving Tess primary custody and Fiona the chance to be raised in a two-parent home—even if that other parent had cheated with his wife. He couldn't blame Tess for that any more than he could blame Kyra for wishing Dugan would die.

Married life hadn't suited him. But fatherhood? He considered Fiona the best part of his life.

He closed up the house and got ready for bed. When he crawled between the sheets, he put on the TV. Most nights he fell asleep to the blue light that flickered across from him. He couldn't manage any other way.

As he started to drift off, the phone charging on his nightstand rang. For the first time in a long time, something other than work popped into his head when he heard the ringing. Had Kyra made it back okay?

He grabbed the phone, which displayed the number from the station.

"McAllister."

The voice ended all thoughts of Kyra and all thoughts of sleep. "You ready, J-Mac? We have another body."

Chapter Sixteen

Kyra wheeled the LAPD vehicle back into the parking lot of the station. On her way there, she'd picked up a bite to eat and had called the hospital where the ambulance had taken Matt. They wouldn't give her any information over the phone, but Jake hadn't called her yet, either.

Although Matt's death would remove one menace from her life, she didn't wish him dead. She still remembered the scared boy lashing out at anything and everyone when she'd been placed with the same foster parents.

She'd been the one person who could communicate with Matt, talk him off the ledge, but he was already too far gone, too far beyond her help when she'd met him. Matt's mother had been a heroin addict, and a long line of her boyfriends and husbands had beaten and abused Matt.

Kyra pushed through the front doors of the station and swiped the back of her hand across her nose. What kind of chance did a boy like that have in this world?

She'd understood him…and he'd understood her. She hoped that Matt survived.

Nodding to the desk sergeant, she said, "I left some things here."

"Go on up. A few people are burning the midnight oil."

Her heart did a backflip. Did that mean Jake was here? Maybe he couldn't sleep. Maybe he wanted to check up on her to make sure she returned the car. It was not like she could or even wanted to steal it.

Could she have trusted Jake enough to tell him she knew about his meeting with Matt and wanted to be there when she questioned him?

She stabbed the elevator button. Why should she trust him? He didn't trust her. He'd been divorced once and through the ringer with another therapist. It didn't take any special skills or training to understand the guy had trust issues. And so did she. A match made in hell.

Not that she was considering a match with Jake. There'd been a moment tonight when she expected a kiss from him, but she'd backed off. She had a feeling once she started kissing Jake McAllister, there would be no turning back.

She stepped into the task force conference room and blinked at the late-night activity. Her gaze jumped to Jake's empty desk.

Billy called across the room. "You looking for J-Mac? He left a while ago."

"No." She had to stop being so obvious. "I left a few things here. What are you doing here so late?"

Billy slumped in his chair and crossed his hands

behind his head. "I'm still trying to ID victim number one. I see her face when I close my eyes."

Billy was a smooth operator, but like Jake, he was a good cop. They did this for the victims, and Billy was doing this for his sister. "None of the working girls around Melrose recognize her?"

"No, and it makes it harder going from a sketch. Her face was in pretty bad shape when we got to her, so we're not showing that around. The sketch artist does a good job, but no hits yet." He rubbed his eyes. Even his typically crisp suit looked wilted.

She took a seat in front of her computer and twisted her head around. "Hey, I heard you're interested in meeting a friend of mine, Megan Wright from KTOP."

Billy's head shot up. "I wouldn't mind an introduction—just to do it right."

"You're not married, are you?"

"Separated." He drew a cross over his heart. "My wife and I aren't living together. We're both free to date."

"Then I'll give Megan your card and put in a good word."

"I appreciate that." The phone on Billy's desk rang and he grabbed it. "Crouch."

Kyra watched his face go hard as he listened to the words on the other end of the line.

"Where? Does J-Mac know?"

Kyra's breath came out in shallow spurts. It had to be another victim.

Billy hung up the phone and steepled his fingers. "The SOB has done it again."

"Another one?" Kyra had wrapped her arms around her body.

"This one dumped in the Ballona Wetlands."

Kyra's arms tightened. "That's...bold. It's not exactly the middle of nowhere like the canyons and trails he's been favoring."

He pushed back from his desk. "I'm heading out there. Do you want to come with me?"

"I'll follow along in my own car, if that's okay. The wetlands are closer to my place—too close."

"I'm leaving now."

"I'll be right behind you."

This time, Kyra left the station to follow an LAPD detective in her own car. She didn't ask Billy if Jake was already at the site. If he wasn't now, he soon would be. Would he be surprised to see her? Irritated?

Forty-five minutes later, she pulled behind Billy's car onto a scene bathed in red-and-white lights. She didn't have to plunge into the trees or hike down a trail. The yellow crime scene tape encircled an area just off the paved walkway through the Ballona Wetlands.

She tugged on Billy's sleeve and pointed to a camera installed on a light post.

He shook his head. "I've already been informed that's broken."

Kyra kicked at a rock, and the long grasses of the wetland tickled her bare legs. She hadn't even gone home yet to change clothes.

Given the hour, the only people shuffling in and out of the area were law enforcement, a few members of the press, including Megan, a few homeless people and a young couple. Had they reported the body?

She knew she wasn't getting close to the crime scene so she sidled up next to Megan. "How'd you hear about this?"

"My guy heard it on the scanner. Young couple called it in. As soon as the Sheriff's Department got here, they knew what they had and reported it to the task force."

"So, she must have the playing card between her lips." Kyra kept her mouth shut about the severed finger. That was not general knowledge.

"And the missing jewelry?" Megan put a finger to her lips. "This is off-the-record, but we've heard reports that the killer is taking jewelry from the victims as a trophy. True or false?"

"That falls under things I can't tell you." Kyra folded her arms in case Megan thought she could wheedle anything out of her.

"This is his fourth victim, all within two months. He's voracious, isn't he?" Megan looked over her shoulder. "And so close to where I live."

"Are you nervous?" Kyra caressed the outline of her gun. Nerves didn't get to her.

"A little. I mean, these victims are a bit younger than I am, but they're not hookers, are they? They're not runaways. They're young women with jobs and school and regular lives."

"Can I give you a piece of advice that I don't want to see on the evening news?"

"Yes."

"Stay away from Melrose Avenue in West Hollywood."

Megan's eyes popped. "For real? Is that where he's picking them up?"

"He's not picking them up there, but let's just say there are some connections to that area that might mean something."

"I swear I'll keep that hush-hush if you promise to give me what you got when the time comes."

"I do." Kyra caught her breath as Jake emerged from the crime scene, the bright lights highlighting the white T-shirt hugging his large frame.

He'd pulled on the same jeans he'd been wearing earlier for his meeting with Matt. It had been the first time she'd seen him out of his suit. The casual clothes suited him better, more in tune with his blatant masculinity.

Megan elbowed her. "There's a hot guy trying to get your attention."

Kyra had been assessing Jake's body so thoroughly she'd missed his cupped hand gesturing to her.

"Speaking of hot guys, Detective Billy Crouch has you in his sights." She slipped Billy's card from her purse and handed it to Megan. "I told him I'd pass along his number."

"Well, thank *you*."

Kyra started toward Jake, who met her halfway.

Of course, he had to get in the first word. "What are you doing here?"

"I was at the station with Billy when he got the news. He invited me along."

He took her arm and whispered in her ear, "Did you get the car back without incident?"

That was not what she expected from his lips with a dead woman in the wetlands. "I did. Is this for sure another victim?"

"Yes. Queen of clubs this time, severed finger, strangulation, no identification. This isn't a fresh kill." He pressed a hand against his chest. "I'm sorry. What I mean is, she was probably killed last night, not tonight. She's far enough off the path to have been missed. This couple had a dog with them, and he discovered the body."

"But so close to civilization. He's getting brazen." She pointed at the camera. "Billy said it's broken."

"It is." Jake scratched at the scruff on his chin. "The killer didn't do it, though. It's been broken for a while, but he must've known that."

"He's thirsty." Kyra sucked in her bottom lip. "You need to stop him because he's not showing any signs of slowing down."

Jake's mouth twisted up at one side. "I know that. I'm waiting for that one mistake, and then we'll close in on him. They all make mistakes."

"The Player never did."

"He did. Even Quinn will tell you he did. Nobody ever picked up on that mistake. The world is a different place than it was twenty years ago. Murder investigations are different. We'll get this guy." The coroner arrived, and Jake turned toward the van. "I need to finish this up. Get home safely—in your own car."

"Got it." She hesitated. "Will I see you at Marissa's

apartment tomorrow? Remember, I'm meeting her roommate, and we're having a look at her jewelry."

"I'll be there." He swung around and disappeared into the tall grasses of the wetlands.

Kyra walked back to her car and waved at Megan getting into her news van. The drive from the Ballona Wetlands to Santa Monica took her less than fifteen minutes at this time of night.

She pulled into her parking spot. As she walked past the dumpster, she studied the ground. She saw a plastic bag that had probably floated from someone's trash, picked it up and slipped it beneath the lid of the dumpster.

Not that she expected another card, with Matt lying in a hospital bed. If Matt was telling the truth and someone had paid him to leave the cards, that person could just as easily pay someone else to do the deed.

But why?

THE FOLLOWING DAY, Kyra saw two clients in the morning and then drove to Marissa Perez's apartment in Reseda, not far from where her abandoned car was found, to meet her roommate, Darcy Myren. Jake had indicated that he'd be late and to start without him.

She pulled alongside the curb in front of a large apartment complex and buzzed the apartment number.

A shaky voice answered the intercom. "Yes?"

"Darcy, this is Kyra Chase. Is this still a good time?"

For her answer, Darcy buzzed open the door, and Kyra stepped into the cool, tiled interior of the apartment building. Neat rows of brass mailboxes lined one wall, facing two elevators.

Kyra went up to the third floor, where Darcy stood at the door of her apartment, waiting for her.

Darcy's dark eyes narrowed. "I thought that cop was coming with you."

"He'll be here later. Is that okay?"

"Yeah, c'mon in." She widened the door for Kyra, and she walked into a place in upheaval.

Kyra raised her eyebrows. "Are you moving?"

"I just can't take it here anymore. I know Marissa wasn't abducted from our place or anything, but it just creeps me out that someone could've been stalking her or watching us."

Kyra's pulse jumped. "Did Marissa ever mention being stalked?"

"No." Darcy placed a hand at her throat. "It's just all too weird. I'm staying with friends now, but I'm moving back in with my parents in Orange County for a while. I can't afford this place on my own, anyway."

"That's probably a good idea. Do you want to talk before Detective McAllister gets here? Then we can look through Marissa's jewelry together."

"Okay." Darcy perched on the edge of a floral couch that had seen better days. "Marissa's sister is coming out from Texas in a few days to pack up her stuff."

"Have you looked through Marissa's things yet?"

"I'm too scared to go into her room."

"I understand." For the next half hour, Kyra allowed Darcy to pour out all her fears and anxieties and paranoia.

By the time the external intercom buzzed, Darcy had cried herself dry.

"Is—is that the detective?"

"Probably. Let him up and go wash your face. I'll meet him."

"Thank you." Darcy dabbed at her wet, swollen eyes. "If I need more help..."

"You can see me again, or I can make a recommendation closer to your parents' place."

Darcy hopped up and answered the intercom, punching the button to allow Jake entrance to the building.

As Darcy retreated to the bathroom, Kyra stood by the door to greet Jake.

He strode down the hallway, his face grim, his muscles tense.

She swallowed and stepped into the hallway. "Everything okay?"

"We identified the victim from last night—Gracie Cho." He shook his head. "Graduated from USC last year."

"Any connection to Melrose yet?"

"Not yet." He pointed to the door. "Everything okay with Darcy?"

"She's very upset. Can't even bring herself to look at Marissa's possessions, but it's a good thing we're here. Marissa's sister is coming out from Texas to pack up her belongings in a few days."

"Then let's get to it."

She let Jake into the apartment just as Darcy was returning with a freshly scrubbed face and a red nose. "Hello."

"Hi, Darcy." He swiveled his head back and forth. "You moving out?"

"Yeah. The landlord's letting me break the lease and everything."

"That's good. Do you want to show us to Marissa's room?"

"This way." She led them down a short hallway and pushed open a door. "Marissa had the master because she made more money than I did and paid more rent."

Jake poked his head into the neat room. "She worked at an advertising agency in Sherman Oaks, didn't she?"

"Yeah, she did online content for them." Darcy sniffed and pointed to a wooden box on top of a dresser. "She kept her jewelry in there, but like I told Kyra, Marissa always wore that jade bracelet. You won't find it there. He took it."

A chill whispered on the back of Kyra's neck. "Let's make sure."

As Darcy hung by the door, Kyra crossed the room to the small dresser littered with makeup, perfume, ticket stubs and all the other accoutrements of a life well lived by a twentysomething young woman.

Kyra flipped up the lid of the box, and stirred her finger through a jumble of costume jewelry. "I don't see a jade bracelet here. Darcy, can you have a look just to make sure?"

"I suppose." Darcy crept toward the dresser as if she expected someone to jump out at her at any moment. Kyra didn't blame her.

Darcy picked through the tangle of necklaces and bracelets, working some pieces loose and setting them on top of the dresser. "Told you. The bracelet's not here."

"Thanks, Darcy. That's helpful." Jake gestured to the door. "Can we talk a little more? Just a few questions that have come up since we last interviewed you."

Darcy beat both of them to the door and resumed her seat on the edge of the couch, looking ready to take flight. "Is it true that this guy gave her a shot of something before strangling her?"

"We think so. You said Marissa didn't use drugs, right?"

"She barely drank." Darcy clutched the arm of the sofa with one hand, her multicolored nails digging into the worn fabric. "Why her?"

"Probably no reason at all." Jake sat on the chair across from Darcy, mimicking her pose on the edge of his seat. "Do you know if Marissa had any reason to be in the West Hollywood area, specifically Melrose Avenue?"

"Melrose?" Darcy's dark brows formed a V over her nose. "No. I mean, maybe we shopped there once or twice, but not often. That stuff's expensive down there."

Jake asked, "She didn't know anyone who worked there? Didn't have any reason to be there for business?"

Her head jerked up. "Is he finding women there?"

"We don't know that for sure. Just checking out a few things."

"Darcy…" Kyra shot a glance at Jake to make sure he didn't have any objections to her asking a question. He gave a slight nod. "Do you know that Marissa had an empty coffee cup from Uncommon Grounds in her car when they found it?"

Darcy's gaze darted from her to Jake. "It doesn't surprise me. Marissa drank a lot of coffee. She had some crazy hours and fueled up on caffeine. Do you think the cup belonged to someone else and not her?"

"No, just wondering if she ever went to the Uncommon Grounds on Melrose."

"Not that I know of. She usually got her coffee from fast-food drive-throughs. If she had a cup from Uncommon Grounds, that probably didn't happen too often."

Jake's phone buzzed in his pocket and he snuck a peek. His stoic face betrayed just one telltale sign—a muscle at the corner of his mouth twitched.

He stood up abruptly. "As always, Darcy, if you remember anything else, give us a call and follow up with Kyra if you need help coping."

"Thanks. I think I'll be better once I move out of here."

Kyra stood up beside Jake and felt his body vibrating next to hers. "Are you okay by yourself now?"

"I have a couple of friends coming over to help me move. I'll be fine. Thanks—and I hope you find this guy."

Outside the apartment, Kyra turned to Jake. "What is it?"

"Something important from the task force. Someone may have seen our guy." He held out his phone. "I'll call Billy when I get to the car."

She had no intention of missing out on this message,

so she dogged his footsteps to his car. He didn't even blink when she got into the passenger seat beside him.

He placed the call and put the phone on Speaker. Billy picked up on the first ring. "J-Mac, aren't you in Reseda at Marissa's apartment?"

"Just finished up there. Whaddya got?" He cleared his throat. "Kyra's listening."

"Perfect. You may need her for this. Once we released Gracie Cho's name today, the task force got a call from a working girl in Hollywood. Two nights ago, she picked up a john who seemed all hopped up on something. They got down to business and the dude had some kinky requests—nothing she hasn't dealt with before, but he did call her Gracie. She didn't think much about it until she saw the name of the victim today. I think we just might have our first sighting of The Copycat Player."

Chapter Seventeen

Jake slammed his fists against the steering wheel. "He slipped up. The bastard slipped up. Give me her info and we'll get right out there."

Kyra grabbed a pen from the console and an envelope from her purse. As Billy recited the name and location of the witness, Kyra jotted it down.

Jake ended the call and cranked on the engine. "Sounds promising as hell."

"That might explain why the killer didn't rape any of his victims." Kyra's knee bounced up and down.

"Didn't want to leave his DNA, but got his kicks with hookers after the murders to satisfy his sick lust."

She clamped her hands on her knees and curled her fingers into the material of her slacks. "If he did this after murdering Gracie, he probably did it after the other killings."

"Maybe Sunny can introduce us to some of her friends." Jake hightailed it to Hollywood and cruised down Hollywood Boulevard, a little tawdry in the light of day.

Kyra squinted at the signs. "She really wants to meet at a hot dog stand?"

"She's not going to give us her address." Jake jabbed his finger at the windshield. "There it is."

"And not even an illegal parking spot available in front."

"I have other tricks up my sleeve." He wheeled the sedan around and pulled into a parking lot that charged five bucks per half hour. He flashed his badge at the parking attendant, who then waved him behind a couple of cars.

"That's—" he turned off the engine "—how it's done."

They walked the half block to the hot dog stand and staked out a table outside under a pink umbrella. She must've been waiting for them because it didn't take Sunny long to spring up from behind a building, her high heels wobbling on the sidewalk as she sashayed toward them.

She definitely had the walk down, but otherwise she could've passed for the girl next door with her slim figure and Bambi eyes. Must've been how Kyra's own mother marketed herself.

Kyra twisted her fingers in her lap and put on a smile for the woman. She had her reasons for doing what she was doing. Kyra was long past judgment.

Jake, ever the gentleman even in the most questionable of circumstances, stood up at her approach. "Sunny?"

Sunny brushed her long hair from her face, lightly

made up for daytime. For all Kyra knew, Sunny could morph into a different persona at night.

"Yeah, I'm Sunny. You Detective McAllister?"

"That's right." He pulled out a plastic chair. "Have a seat."

"Who's she?" Sunny aimed a short pink-tipped fingernail at Kyra.

"She's a victims' rights advocate. She's working with me on the case."

"Good." Sunny dragged the chair back and squirmed into it. "Because I'm a victim here, right? Dude could've killed me, too."

"Why don't you start from the beginning." Jake pulled out a notebook. "Tell me how you met him, what he said, how he looked. If this seems credible, I'll get you down to the station to meet with a sketch artist."

"Credible? You mean like believable?" Sunny tapped one finger on the table. "This is the real deal."

"So, how did you meet this guy and what time?" Jake held his pen poised over the paper.

"Wait. Can I at least get lunch out of this?"

"Sure." He pocketed his notepad. "What would you like?"

"Get me the Hollywood Dog and a lemonade."

"Kyra?" Jake raised his eyebrows at her.

"Same."

He rose from the table and got in line behind two tourists in shorts, clutching maps to the stars' homes.

Sunny narrowed her brown eyes. "He's fine. Probably doesn't have to pay for it, but sometimes that doesn't matter, you know?"

Kyra nodded.

"You'd be surprised at who comes knocking at my door." Sunny held up her fingers and began ticking off the various professions of men who found themselves in need of her services. She'd just gotten to politicians when Jake returned to the table with three dogs and three drinks.

The Hollywood Dog boasted chili, raw onions and corn chips, and Sunny sank her white teeth into the end of the whole mess.

A few more bites and several napkins later, she got down to business. "Okay, this happened the night before last. I was working my corner when this man approached me for, you know, a good time."

"What time?"

"After midnight. I usually work until two when the bars close."

"What did he look like?"

"Average height. I'm about five foot eight with my heels on, and he was a little taller than me. Average weight, not buff or anything." She eyed Jake's shoulders, her gaze slipping to his strong forearms resting on the table.

"Hair?"

"Longish. Below his ears." Sunny drew a line across her neck. "But shaved up on one side. Brown. Brown eyes. Glasses. No facial hair."

"Did you see a car?"

"He approached me on foot. Wanted the full package, so I took him to one of the motel rooms we use."

Jake hunched forward. "Do you remember which one?"

"Before you get all excited, because I know what you're after, he didn't leave any prints in that room because he was wearing gloves."

Kyra blurted out, "Gloves? It had to be over seventy degrees the other night."

"I know, right?" Sunny spread her hands. "That was the first weirdo thing."

"What were the rest of the weirdo things?" Jake slurped down some of his drink.

"He wanted me to lie still with my hands at my sides. He didn't want me touching him." She shrugged. "Hey, less work for me, right? He also put his hand around my neck. Lotta guys do that."

Kyra had to put down her hot dog and swallow fast as the food turned to ashes in her mouth. That alone should terrify Sunny.

"Then he started calling me Gracie. Gracie this. Gracie that."

Jake glanced at Kyra. "Do you remember what he said to Gracie?"

"Not really. Mumbling pathetic things like, how do you like me now, Gracie? Stuff like that. Like he was getting something over on her." Sunny popped the last of her hot dog in her mouth and brushed her hands together. "Couldn't end fast enough for me. He paid with cash and left. Didn't think about him again until this afternoon when I heard the name of one of those victims of The Copycat Player—Gracie. Freaked me out. I mean it's not a common name, am I right?"

"You're right." Jake slipped Sunny his card. "Can you come to the station to sit down with an artist? We'd like to get this sketch out as soon as possible."

"Really?" Sunny toyed with her rings. "Nobody's gonna know it's me, right?"

Jake raised two fingers. "Complete anonymity."

"Then I'll do it. Can you give me a ride?"

"One more thing." Jake crumpled the waxy yellow paper from his hot dog and lobbed it into a trash can. "You said he didn't leave prints in the room because he wore gloves. Did he leave his…DNA anywhere?"

"His DNA?" Sunny rolled her eyes. "You mean his—"

Jake cut in. "Exactly."

"You know—" Sunny tapped her nails on the plastic table "—now that you mention it, he was my last trick of the night. I always head home after the last one to shower at my own place. I haven't done laundry since then, so the clothes I was wearing that night just might have some of his…DNA."

"Yes!" Jake slammed his fist on the table, rattling the ice in their drinks. "That's what I wanted to hear. Is your place nearby? Can we stop by there on our way to the station?"

"Sure." Sunny dabbed her lips with a napkin and picked up her cup. "You really think this might be the guy?"

"Right now, it's the best we got."

After swinging by Sunny's apartment, where she ran inside and returned to the car with a garbage bag full of clothes, Jake drove on to the station and set Sunny up with a sketch artist. He then had one of the officers on the task force bag Sunny's clothes for a trip to the lab.

When he finally collapsed behind his desk, he raised his eyes to the ceiling. "I have a good feeling about this."

Kyra left her own desk to join him. Maybe Brandon should've put her right next to him instead of across the room. "Do you have other task force members questioning some of the other hookers in the area to see if any of them had similar experiences?"

"They're on it." Jake massaged his temples. "He thought he was being so smart by not sexually assaulting his victims and leaving DNA, but he messed up by mentioning Gracie's name. They always mess up."

"The Player never did." Kyra squeezed the back of her neck.

"He did, Kyra. Somehow, some way, he did mess up. Nobody caught it."

"Quinn would've caught it." Heat rose to her cheeks at the tone of her voice. Quinn didn't need her to defend him.

Jake's hand dropped to her thigh. "Helluva detective, but even he'd tell you he missed something. There is no perfect crime."

Her gaze dropped to his hand, and he snatched it away. "I'm sorry."

"Don't be. You don't have to…" She zipped her lips as Billy entered the room.

He rushed over and high-fived Jake. "I think we got this, my man. Thank the heavens for working girls—

I mean that from a law enforcement perspective, of course."

"Of course." Jake snorted. "Sunny's still with the artist and her clothes are being tested as we speak. Rush job on that."

Billy said, "I also sent out a team to look for cameras along Sunny's stretch of turf. Maybe we can get this guy on camera, too. Maybe catch sight of a car."

Kyra scooted Billy's chair away from Jake and stood up. "All yours."

"Didn't mean to chase you off, especially since I got a call from Megan today."

"Oh, good." Kyra shook her finger at Billy. "Treat her right. She's coming out of a bad breakup."

"I treat all the ladies right."

"That's your problem." Jake shoved a file toward Billy. "We're tracking down Gracie's last movements. We don't see a Melrose connection yet, but we're not ruling it out. We're also looking for missing jewelry because Marissa's jade bracelet is definitely gone."

One of the officers from the task force called across the room. "Kyra, can I talk to you a minute?"

She left Jake and Billy, heads bent over the file, and approached the officer. "What do you need?"

"Gracie Cho's parents don't speak English, just Korean. We'd like to get someone to help them out. Can you recommend someone?"

"I think so. Are they here in LA?"

"Yes."

"Let me reach out to my contacts. I'll let you know."

For the next hour before the task force meeting, Kyra

stayed on the phone searching for a Korean-speaking therapist or grief counselor. She located one minutes before Jake stood up and announced the meeting.

As they all crowded into the conference room; Kyra stood at the back as she always did. Though the team seemed to accept her, she'd caught a few looks from the other officers as she accompanied Jake through the halls of the station. They couldn't accuse her of currying favor with the boss since their jobs and hers were on different planes, but she and Jake didn't need the gossip.

As Jake started the slides, the first one up contained the sketch based on Sunny's description. As Kyra studied the eyes behind the glasses, she shivered. They looked so mild, yet they had an emptiness about them. She could only guess that they took on a different look when he was hunting his prey. His longish brown hair cut shorter on one side was distinctive, though not distinctive enough for the Hollywood or Melrose crowd— if that's where he hung out. That clean-cut barista at Uncommon Grounds was the exception not the rule in that area.

She shifted her focus to Billy, now doing the talking.

"We didn't find a Melrose connection to Gracie. She lived in Encino and worked in Studio City, but we're not done yet. Still no ID on the woman found at the Malibu fire site, so that hurts us for clues. We're asking Sunny, the hooker who gave us the sketch, to put out the word among her girls to step up if they had an encounter like hers and we just might get DNA from Sunny's unwashed clothing she wore the night of her encounter with the man talking about Gracie. Sorry, no prints, Clive." Billy waved to the fingerprint technician standing in the back with Kyra. "We're in the best shape we've been in yet. So, keep up the canvassing of the Melrose and Hollywood areas. We need to get him before he kills again."

The meeting adjourned, and Brandon placed a stack of the sketches on a table at the exit. As Kyra wandered out, she grabbed a couple.

Back in the war room, Jake stopped by her desk. "Billy and I are headed out for a few more interviews, and then I have a meeting with Castillo before I knock off. Do you need a ride back to your car? You left it at Marissa's apartment."

"If you're going to Hollywood, that's out of your way. Don't worry. I'll get it."

He leaned in close to her. "I just don't want you stealing another car."

She smiled. "I'll get a rideshare."

"I didn't get a chance to tell you earlier. I called the hospital and Matt's still in a coma. Doesn't look good."

Her bottom lip quivered. "I'm not going to pretend I didn't have problems with him, but he was the closest thing I had to a brother."

"No more cards, though?"

"No."

"He was probably lying about getting paid." Jake rapped his knuckles on her desk. "Thanks for coming out with me today to talk to Sunny. I think it helped having you there. The working girls are always suspicious of cops."

"Happy to help, although you did all the talking."

"Have a good night…and be careful."

"I always am." She was lying, and he knew it.

Kyra worked for another hour, but it was still light when Rachel Blackburn called her.

"I hate to bother you, Kyra, but can you meet me before I head home?"

"Of course. Where?"

"You can just come by the shop. I'm closing at eight."

"That's perfect. I have to pick up my car first. I'll see you around eight."

Kyra gathered her belongings and ordered an app car from her phone. She slung her bag over her shoulder and hurried out to the curb in front of the station.

When her ride pulled behind her car near Marissa's apartment, the sun was beginning to set. The strident oranges and reds produced by the haze from the wildfire had subsided to a creamy vanilla orange Popsicle marking the end of the Indian summer. It felt like the closing of a chapter. Maybe that meant the task force would close in on The Copycat Player.

Kyra paused before she got in her car and gazed at the building across the street. Those young women had probably been full of excitement and big dreams when they moved into that place. Now that chapter had ended, too.

She made it to West Hollywood just about ten minutes past eight and lucked out with a metered parking spot on the street. The Closed sign hung in the window of the shop where Rachel worked, so Kyra cupped her hand over her eyes and peered through the glass.

Rachel, behind the counter, waved and held up a finger.

Kyra waited on the sidewalk like a buoy, interrupting the flow of the pedestrian wave that surged around her.

Rachel stepped outside and locked the door. Turning toward Kyra, she dropped her keys in her purse. "Thanks for coming out. I'm doing okay, but locking up at night always got to me, even before my phone was stolen by a serial killer."

"I can understand that. Do you want to sit somewhere?"

"Uncommon Grounds? They're open until ten."

As they walked through the door of the coffeehouse, Kyra said, "You know, we think your phone was lifted here, maybe when you were waiting for your coffee."

"That could be, and it makes me feel a little better. It means I probably wasn't targeted specifically, just a crime of opportunity."

Kyra's lips twitched.

"What?" Rachel nudged her arm. "Why are you laughing?"

"I'm not laughing. Jake... Detective McAllister was right about you. You've got good instincts." Kyra pulled out her wallet. "It's on me."

When they got to the counter, the clean-cut guy from the other day took their order. Kyra glanced at his name tag. "Still here, huh?"

"Ma'am?" Jordy tilted his head, his dark, rather close-set eyes making him look like a bird.

"Oh, I'm sorry. You probably see hundreds of people all day. I was in the other afternoon and you mentioned you don't always work at this store because you don't look the part. It's the hair."

"Did I?" His brow furrowed. "I'm sorry. I don't remember."

"That's all right. I'd like a peach iced tea and…"

Rachel ordered her frothy concoction and they stepped to the side after Kyra paid for their drinks.

Kyra tapped the counter that lined up against the window. "There are charging stations here and everything. We figured you may have set down your phone or plugged it in and forgotten it."

"I don't know about charging it, but I do have a habit of carrying it in my hand and then putting it down, so it's possible." She sighed. "Anybody could've picked it up in here."

Rachel already knew about Kelsey's connection to Melrose, as she'd had her nose piercing done by Gustavo in the shop, but she didn't know about the Uncommon Grounds coffee cup in Marissa's car. Of course, that cup could've come from a number of Uncommon Grounds sprinkled around the city.

Rachel tugged on Kyra's purse strap. "Can you get the coffees? A table by the window just opened up. I'm going to grab it for us."

Kyra nodded as Rachel spun around to nab the prime table. There seemed to be just as many people using this place as their office during the night as there were during the day.

When her name was called, Kyra picked up both drinks and carried them to the table where Rachel was texting. "New phone?"

"I gave up on ever finding my other phone, and I don't know if I'd want to use it if I did." Rachel hunched her shoulders. "Everything was backed up on the cloud, so I was able to restore all my stuff."

"The wonders of technology." Kyra reached into her bag and pulled out the composite drawing of Sunny's john. She flattened it on the table. "We have a sketch of someone of interest to the case. Have you seen this guy around here?"

Rachel smoothed her hand across the face. "He kind of looks familiar, facially, but I'd remember someone with that hair…even here on Melrose." She picked it up and held it close to her face. "Can I keep this?"

"Of course. I have others. Ask Gustavo." Kyra stirred some sweetener into her tea. "Tell me what's worrying you."

Rachel recited some of her fears and tried to brush them off. But this hadn't been her first encounter with the seedy side of LA and she'd been feeling rattled.

They chatted for almost an hour until the talk turned toward Rachel's future employment. "I already applied for the dispatcher job, and Detective McAllister said he'd make sure my app gets fast-tracked."

"That's great. Have you followed up with him?"

"No, do you think that's okay?"

"He'd expect it." Kyra tapped her cup. "Do you want another?"

"No, but I am going to hit the ladies' room."

When Rachel left the table, Kyra picked up her cup and swiped her thumb through the moisture on the outside. The blue print circling around the cup listed the locations of Uncommon Grounds in the LA metro area. Her finger traced a line through West Hollywood and trailed to Studio City.

Gracie worked in Studio City. Marissa, who had a cup from Uncommon Grounds in her car, worked in Sherman Oaks, next to Studio City. Kelsey had gotten her nose pierced here on Melrose, steps from Uncommon Grounds, and Rachel most likely had her phone stolen from this shop. Three of the four victims had a connection to areas with Uncommon Grounds. West Hollywood. Studio City.

Kyra plunged her hand into her purse, which was hanging on the back of her chair, and dragged out another composite sketch. Why would a killer with a distinctive hairstyle like this visit a prostitute after one of his crimes? One who wasn't afraid of being caught? That didn't describe The Copycat Player. Did he even realize he'd been saying Gracie's name?

Someone touched Kyra's shoulder, and she jumped and turned her head.

"Sorry." Rachel squeezed her shoulder. "I thought I was the jittery one. I'm going to take off now. Are you ready?"

Kyra covered the sketch with her arm. "Actually, I'm going to hang out and make a few phone calls."

She scooted back her chair. "Do you want me to walk you to your car?"

"No, I'm good. There are still a lot of people roaming around, and my car's in a public lot." She bent over and gave Kyra a one-armed hug. "Thanks so much. I'm sorry I'm such a wuss."

"Don't be ridiculous. Call me anytime."

Rachel waved at the door and plunged into the steady stream of people on the sidewalk.

Kyra placed the drawing in front of her again. Maybe he'd worn a disguise for Sunny. The hair. She covered the unique cut with her hand and looked at the face. The glasses. She blotted out the lens on one eye with her fingers.

Then her heart slammed against her chest. She recognized that face. Had just seen it.

Chapter Eighteen

As the meeting with Castillo wound down, Jake checked the time on his phone and saw several missed text messages and phone calls. He squeezed the back of his neck. He hadn't had a good night's sleep in days, but the hard work was paying off. The lab found male DNA on Sunny's underwear, and they'd start running it through CODIS tomorrow. If Sunny's john had been arrested for a felony before, he'd be in the system and they'd have their first real suspect.

Captain Castillo went around the room, but everyone was too eager to get out of there to bring up anything else to discuss on the case. They'd have a whole new ball game tomorrow.

As soon as Castillo adjourned the meeting, almost everyone in the room reached for their phones, which Castillo had demanded be silent for the duration of the meeting.

Jake's stomach demanded food, so he took a quick leave of everyone and headed to his car. He got behind the wheel and listened to his first voice mail.

A sheriff's deputy from the West Hollywood division had talked to a streetwalker who echoed Sunny's account with her weird john. Jake called him back.

"Yates, this is McAllister. What do you have on the hooker? Same guy?"

"Sounds like the same guy. Same night as Kelsey's murder, and she thinks he was saying a name but she doesn't remember if it was Kelsey or not."

"That sounds promising. Will she come in and make a statement?"

"She will, but I'm not sure it's the same guy. I showed her the composite, and she said he looked similar but she can guarantee he didn't have hair like that."

Jake ran a thumb along his jaw. "Different hair?"

"And she thinks her guy had a mustache or some kind of facial hair."

"Give me her contact info, and I'll have her come in for an interview and a session with the sketch artist. If they're the same facially, he might be wearing a disguise. He's being careful."

Jake ended the call and pulled out the sketch. He grabbed a pen from his console and drew in a more normal haircut for the man. The face looked even more familiar than it had when he'd first seen the rendering.

Propping it up on his steering wheel, he went back to his phone and returned a call from Billy.

"Sorry, man. I was in one of Castillo's meetings. You know how that goes."

"Mind-numbing." Billy took a sip of something. "We got a little more info on Gracie's habits. She worked in Studio City. Wasn't known to frequent West Hollywood or Melrose at all. So, that's a blank. Looks like she's missing a ring, which I think we can now deduce is his trophy."

"You're right." Jake drummed his thumbs on the steering wheel. "Coffee?"

"Huh?"

"Any coffee cups in Gracie's car, like Marissa's?"

"I didn't process her car, but I can check on the photos. I did tell you there was no way to tell if Marissa's cup came from the Uncommon Grounds in West Hollywood or some other store, right?"

"Yeah, but I'd like to know about Gracie."

"On it. You still at the station?"

"In my car going through my phone. I'm starving. You wanna get something to eat?"

"I'm meeting up with Megan Wright tonight after she does the ten-o'clock news. Tell me that's not sexy?"

"Watch you don't cozy up too much to the press."

Billy chuckled. "That's exactly what I plan to do, my brother. If you can make an exception for a therapist, I can make one for a reporter."

"Whatever. Text me the info on the contents of the car, if you get it."

"Will do. Go eat."

Jake listened to one more voice mail, this one from Rachel Blackburn.

"Hello, Detective McAllister. I just wanted to know if you saw my application come through for dispatcher. I—I just had coffee with Kyra, and she told me it was okay for me to check with you."

Jake sent Rachel a text, indicating he'd seen her app and flagged it for Personnel.

Then he cranked on the engine with the intent to take Billy's advice, and headed to an all-night diner not too far from his place.

As he sat at the Formica table in a booth to himself, he placed his phone in front of him. He had one more voice mail, which he'd been avoiding. After he ordered some meat loaf, he tapped the final voice mail from the hospital where Matt Dugan lay in a coma.

He listened to the news of Dugan's passing and gulped down some water. Should he tell Kyra now? She'd seemed almost sad about Dugan's condition, but she'd be relieved he wouldn't be around to make her life hell anymore...or to tell her secrets.

Molly, who'd been working at this diner for the past twenty years, placed his food in front of him. "I had the cook get you an extra slice of meat loaf, J-Mac. You look like you could use it."

"Thanks, Molly." He dug into the closest thing he'd had to a home-cooked meal in weeks, savoring every bite until his phone buzzed again.

He glanced at the text from Billy, who must be pouring on the cologne in anticipation of his hot date by now. He wiped his hands on a napkin and tapped his phone.

He read the text aloud to no one. "Coffee cup from Uncommon Grounds in Gracie's car."

Jake's fingertips buzzed as he opened the attachment. He studied the photo of the inside of Gracie's car, which had been left on the street near the house of a friend she was supposed to visit the night she was murdered. The coffee cup sat in the cup holder, a smear of pink lipstick on the lid.

With a pulse throbbing in his temple, Jake dug into the bag he'd brought into the diner with him and stashed on the seat beside him. He pulled out a blank sheet of paper and smacked it down on the tabletop next to his empty plate.

As he'd done many times before, he wrote three names across the top—Marissa, Kelsey and Gracie. They still had no ID on the first victim or a car, but he knew Billy would die trying to give that woman a name. Beneath Marissa's name, he wrote that she had a coffee cup from Uncommon Grounds in her car and worked near Studio City. Under Kelsey's name, he wrote that she'd frequented Melrose Boulevard where an Uncommon Grounds was located. Now, under Gracie's name he could add that she worked in Studio City and had a cup from Uncommon Grounds in her car.

The coffee place could link all three women, although they couldn't be sure Kelsey went to Uncommon Grounds on Melrose. Same coffeehouse but two different locations—West Hollywood and Studio City. That wasn't much of a link.

He tugged on his ear. How had he known about Uncommon Grounds in Studio City? He scrambled in his bag for the altered sketch of Sunny's client and dragged it out, placing it next to his scribbled chart of the three victims.

His nostrils flared with the shot of adrenaline that rushed through his body. He'd known about Uncommon Grounds in Studio City because a barista in West Hollywood had told him about it.

The barista who'd worked in both places and had an uncanny resemblance to the composite sketch.

"JORDY, RIGHT?" Kyra put on her most understanding therapist smile although her heart was thundering in her chest.

The fresh-faced young man glanced up from wiping the counter, his eyes taking a few seconds to focus on her. "Yes?"

"I was wondering if you could check in the back for more scones." She tapped the glass display case of bakery goods. "It looks like you're out, but I'm hoping you have some left. I'll even take old ones or frozen ones, if you can heat them up."

His features seemed to rearrange themselves on his face, as if sampling a few expressions until he found the right one—friendly, mild annoyance. "None of our items are frozen. All fresh daily."

"Ah, that's why they're so yummy. Can you please check for me?"

His brown eyes shifted around the mostly empty store, which he'd been prepping for closing. "I suppose I can check."

"That would be great. Thanks."

Jordy stashed his towel beneath the counter and made for the back.

As soon as he disappeared, Kyra dashed to the other end of the counter, the pickup area, and hoisted herself across the counter to grab the cup Jordy had been sipping from for the past ten minutes.

What if he saw his sketch in circulation and took off? She could at least grab a sample of his DNA before that happened. She dropped his cup into her bag, which she'd left gaping open and slithered back to her side of the counter, landing on her tiptoes.

She turned to survey the other customers, all too busy packing up their gear, finishing their conversations and getting that last bit of work in before returning to their homes to notice her actions.

She smoothed back her hair just as Jordy returned from the back empty-handed. "Sorry. We don't have any scones left. Can I get you something else?"

"That's okay. Thanks for checking." She pivoted, clutching her bag against her body and charging for the door. He'd already flipped the sign to Closed.

The nighttime air hit her hot cheeks and she walked toward her car on legs she hadn't realized were trembling. She dipped her fingers into the side pouch of her purse for her keys, sweeping from side to side in the narrow space.

She stopped and zipped open the large compartment of her purse. Her hand clawed through her wallet, makeup bag, a small notebook and a bottle of ibuprofen. She shook the purse, listening for the distinctive jingle of her key chain.

Panic gripped the back of her neck with a cold hand. Had she left them in Uncommon Grounds? She couldn't go back there now. What if Jordy noticed his cup missing behind the counter? He'd link it to her request for scones.

She took a deep breath, her gaze taking in the nightspots on Melrose still open on a weeknight. She could slip into one of the restaurants, call Jake and wait for him there.

He wouldn't be too thrilled with her amateur sleuthing, but he'd be happy to get Jordy's DNA once she told him her suspicions—especially once they got the DNA from Sunny's clothing tomorrow.

Another thought seized her imagination. Jordy could have her keys. He'd been near her and Rachel a few times, mopping the floor and wiping down tables.

She took a deep breath. He wasn't going to steal her car, and he wasn't going to wait for her at her apartment. He didn't know where she lived and wouldn't get it from her registration in the car. Quinn had cautioned her long ago to black out the address on her registration just in case someone did steal her car. With the blacked-out address, the thief wouldn't know where she lived...and neither would Jordy.

Unless he already knew. Had Matt really left those cards at her apartment and car?

She placed a call to Jake and it flipped to voice mail. "Jake, I'm on Melrose, just left Uncommon Grounds. I had some suspicions about that barista who works there and I managed to take something of his, but now I don't have my keys. Long story. Meet me at The Ripe Tomato. I think they're open until eleven."

She ended the call and hustled to the corner to wait for the light to cross the street. When she got to the other side, she waited for a group of people leaving the restaurant and coming right at her. She stopped and moved to the side.

As she did so, someone came up behind her. She felt warm breath on the back of her neck and then a sharp pinch into her flesh.

Gasping, she spun around—right into the arms of Jordy.

He grabbed her around the waist and draped an arm over her shoulder. "Whoa, too much to drink?"

She stumbled against him, inhaling the scent of coffee grounds on his clothing. Why was she thinking about coffee grounds? She fumbled for her gun pouch with thick fingers, but Jordy easily removed the purse from her grasping hands.

"I'll take that. You have something else of mine, too, don't you? So nice, so friendly. They all pretend to be nice and friendly." His hand plunged into her open purse and grabbed the cup.

At least he hadn't noticed the gun tucked in the pouch. Her tongue felt twice its size as she attempted to form words being transmitted slowly from her fuzzy brain.

He laughed. "Yeah, she had one too many."

He guided her along the sidewalk, which had turned into a tunnel.

She could barely focus on her feet tripping over the pavement, Jordy's arm propping her up, Jordy propelling her to the same fate as her mother.

"No."

"It's okay. I pumped enough drugs into your system,

you'll hardly notice when the world stops turning for you." He continued to march her along, and she was happy for him to do so, as she could barely feel her legs.

She could still feel the occasional brush of another human and hear voices far off at the end of the tunnel. He didn't have her alone, yet.

Then she heard the jingle of keys, the beep of a horn. His car.

"No." The word screamed in her head, but came out like a whimper.

Jordy mumbled something.

"What?" The word sounded like a wisp of air.

"Rule number four. The victim should never be someone you know. Rule number four. Rule number four."

She put all her efforts into forming words with her mouth and tongue. "You know me, Jordy. I know you."

"None of you know me. You pretend you do. Get muffins, Jordy. Get scones, Jordy. Get decaf, half-whip, low-fat, extra foam, shot on the side, Jordy." He maneuvered her to the passenger side of his car, and she couldn't move her limbs to fight him off, couldn't reach her weapon, couldn't get away.

"Rule number four. Rule number four."

"You're violating rule number four, Jordy."

Had he heard her mumbled words?

He propped her against the car and opened the door. Once he got her in his car, he'd strangle her, dump her body and hook up with a prostitute.

"Rule number four. Rule number four," Jordy sobbed as he grabbed her to shove her into the car.

"Stop, Jordy. It's over. Let her go."

Jordy dropped his hands from her body, and she slid halfway down the car.

Had she imagined Jake's voice in her fog. "Jake?"

Jordy ducked and reached into the car. "Get back. I'll kill her if you don't get back."

"Let her go, Jordy. It's over. I called for backup. More cops than you can imagine are going to be rolling up any second."

The scream of sirens punctuated Jake's words, and Kyra hugged the side of the car to stay upright. It was over. She wasn't going to die like her mother.

Jordy grabbed her around the neck and dragged her backward, a cold blade at her neck. "I said I'd kill her, and I will. It doesn't matter anymore. Nothing matters anymore. I broke rule number four."

Kyra bucked against Jordy's hold, creating a sliver of space between them. In that split second, a blast of gunfire cracked through the air.

Wet droplets sprayed her face as Jordy released his grip on her and crumpled to the ground at her feet. She staggered back, her hand sliding against the blood-splattered car window.

Jake rushed to her side, his weapon drawn, the smell of gunpowder permeating the air. He nudged Jordy's body with his foot, and the unlikely killer rolled onto his back, the knife resting on his outstretched palm.

As several squad cars flooded the area, illuminating the sky with their revolving red-and-blue lights, Jake curled a hand around her waist, burying his face in her hair.

"Kyra! Are you all right? Tell me you're all right." He smoothed a rough hand down her throat.

She swallowed and mumbled, "He drugged me, but I'm fine. He didn't cut me."

Jake must've understood her because he gathered her in his arms and pressed his lips against her temple. "Thank God, you're safe. I thought I'd lost you. I thought I'd reacted too slowly."

Several cops rushed in, weapons drawn, but Kyra had eyes for only one cop. As she rested her head against his shoulder, she said, "You were just in time."

Epilogue

"Kyra said one beer, Quinn."

The gruff detective snorted. "Just because she solved her first murder case, she thinks she can boss us around."

Kyra placed a bottle of beer in front of Quinn. "If I hadn't gotten ahead of myself and had just left Uncommon Grounds without playing amateur sleuth and called Jake about my suspicions, which he already had, maybe the task force could've arrested Jordy Lee Cannon without fanfare and gotten some answers out of him."

Jake grabbed the plates of fish and chips and brought them to the coffee table. "I don't know what we could've gotten out of him. We know how he met his victims—at Uncommon Grounds in West Hollywood and Studio City. They weren't alarmed when he approached them because they knew him from the coffee place or he looked vaguely familiar to them. He plunged a needle into their necks to disable them, got them in his car where he finished them off by strangulation and then dumped their bodies. He maybe tried to throw us off by mimicking The Player's MO, and he took a piece of jewelry for a trophy—we found all the items in his room at his mother's house."

"But not the fingers." Quinn picked up a fry, considered it and popped it into his mouth.

Jake chewed the inside of his mouth. "Maybe he never wanted the fingers as trophies. He just took them to copy The Player and got rid of them."

"To catching the bad guy." Kyra held up her beer, and Jake and Quinn toasted with her, clinking the necks of their bottles.

She said, "He sure seemed upset about breaking rule number four."

Quinn raised his shaggy eyebrows and Jake said, "We think rule number four was not knowing your victim. Jordy figured he was following rule number four because he didn't really know these women. We wouldn't have been able to find out about Jordy by tracing the victims' friends or family. But he knew he'd broken that rule because he didn't choose random victims. He chose women he knew through Uncommon Grounds."

Kyra shook some vinegar over her fish and chips. "I didn't realize serial killers had sets of rules."

"Of course they do." Quinn glanced at Jake. "Did you find his rules or anything like that when you searched his mother's house?"

"Nope. He must've had them in his head. I wonder what the other rules encompassed."

"Obviously, not leaving prints or DNA. He wore gloves and he didn't sexually assault his victims."

Quinn shook his head. "A careful killer...just like The Player."

Kyra hunched her shoulders. "I'm just glad you found Jordy's car so fast when you got to Melrose."

"His manager told me where he parked. When Rachel mentioned that the two of you had met for coffee that night and then you left that message about finding something, I got a sinking feeling in my gut. I'm just glad I got there on time. I'd shoot that guy all over again and damn his interview or any lies he could tell us."

Kyra gave him a look from beneath her lashes that made him glad all over again.

She brushed her fingers together. "At least Billy ID'd the first victim, so we didn't need Jordy's help with that."

"Why did that take so long?" Quinn crunched into a piece of battered fish.

"Shelby Shipton was from out of town. She'd pulled up stakes in Idaho and came out to LA to make a new life and pursue her dreams."

"Sounds like someone else I know." Quinn reached over and grabbed Kyra's hand. "I heard about Matt Dugan's death. Are you okay?"

Kyra shifted her gaze from Quinn to Jake and back to Quinn's face again. "I—I was sorry to hear about Matt. He took a bad road a long time ago, so it's not surprising."

Quinn squeezed Kyra's fingers in his gnarled ones. "He won't bother you anymore."

She sniffed and took a gulp of beer.

Was the sadness feigned? Jake knew all too well you could mourn the loss of someone you didn't like.

They finished their food, and he helped Kyra clean up the kitchen while Quinn watched TV. The old detective had gotten a supreme sense of satisfaction when they caught The Copycat Player—must've been almost as good as solving the original. Almost.

Kyra wiped her hands on a dish towel and snapped him with it. "Do you want to go outside and watch the sunset from the bridge?"

"Sounds good." He called into the living room. "Quinn, you wanna go out with us?"

Quinn waved his hand. "You two go. I'm watching my show. I like to laugh at all the stupid things these detectives do—and the public really believes things work that way."

Kyra poked Jake in the side. "You should watch a great movie called *Shots Fired*, Quinn. True to life."

Jake rolled his eyes. She'd never let him forget that...and he hoped she'd keep on reminding him.

With a last glance at Quinn, Kyra opened the front door and stepped onto the porch.

Jake inhaled the scent of the ocean. "It's pretty out here."

"Not quite like Venice, Italy, but not like LA, either."

When they got to the bridge, they sat down, dangling their legs over the water. Jake slipped an arm around her shoulders, and she leaned into him. They hadn't had a real date yet, but what they'd been through together had brought them closer than a hundred *real* dates could.

He pinched her chin with his fingers and kissed her sweet lips, just a little tart from the lemon. But that was Kyra—sweet and tart.

When he pulled away, she stroked his jaw with her fingertips. "Does this mean you don't hate therapists anymore?"

"Never did." He rubbed her back, which arched like a cat's beneath his touch. "I'm liking *this* therapist a lot right now."

The phone next to him on the wooden bridge buzzed, and he groaned. "The pitfalls of dating a cop. My ex-wife never got used to it."

"I'm not your ex." Kyra swept up the phone and handed it to him. "It's Billy."

"Hey, Billy. You're interrupting my private time."

"I didn't know you had any of that, brother." Billy coughed. "You're gonna want to hear this—or maybe not."

"What is it?" A slow dread thrummed through Jake's veins.

"Body just discovered—card in the mouth and severed little finger."

Jake's gut knotted as he grabbed Kyra's hand.

"What's wrong, Jake?"

"Looks like we have another copycat killer."

* * * * *

Look for **The Decoy,** *the next book in*
A Kyra and Jake Investigation series
from Carol Ericson, available next month wherever
Harlequin Intrigue books are sold!